HER BROKEN BILLIONAIRE BOSS

A CLEAN BILLIONAIRE ROMANCE BOOK THREE

BREE LIVINGSTON

Edited by
CHRISTINA SCHRUNK

Her Broken Billionaire Boss

Copyright © 2018 by **Bree Livingston**

Edited by Christina Schrunk

https://www.facebook.com/christinaschrunk.editor

Proofread by Krista R. Burdine

https://www.facebook.com/iamgrammaresque

Cover design by Victorine Lieske

http://victorinelieske.com/

Bree Livingston

https://www.breelivingston.com

Her Broken Billionaire Boss / Bree Livingston. -- 1st ed.

ISBN: 9781983200915

To my readers: From the bottom of my heart, thank you for continuing to read my stories. Hearing that you love them makes my day. I love this story. Liam and Sara are so cute. I hope you love them too.

I'd like to say thanks to my cat for not spilling water on my laptop. He gave me the evil eye, which in Skittles land, is give me my demands or the electronic gets it. I guess thanks isn't the right word choice, but we'll go with it.

A heartfelt thanks to my editor and proofreader who helped make this book better than it started out.

And lastly, to my family who still aren't convinced we need a housekeeper. I'll keep pushing for it, just so you know.

$\mathcal{L}$iam Thomas spun his wheelchair around in the living room, nearly clipping his sister. "Watch it." He wished she'd stop following him. He didn't want to talk anymore. Why couldn't she leave him alone?

"You watch it," Kimberly said, pushing her classic red hair—the same as his own—over her shoulder. They were also equally stubborn. "You're the one in the wheelchair, so you're the one who should be careful."

She was driving him nuts. On top of getting ready for her wedding in a week and then a subsequent honeymoon, now she was trying to have a nurse stay with him while she was gone. "I'm not having a nurse stay here. I don't need a nurse." Liam crossed his arms over his chest.

"What happens if you fall or something? This house is on the side of a Denver mountain. It's the middle of winter. You need someone here. Unless, of course, you're just faking still being injured, in which case I'd be happy to let you stay here alone." She smiled.

His Adam's apple bobbed as he swallowed. She'd seemed to suspect for a while he'd been faking it, but he wasn't ready to come clean. "My hip is killing me."

Her eyebrows went up, and she blinked. "The doctor says it's completely healed."

"Well, it's not. It hurts. You think I'd be in this stupid thing if it was healed?" Liam didn't want to lie, but there were things he didn't want to face yet, and they were worse.

"Then you can't stay by yourself. I can't risk you getting hurt again."

Liam's head dropped back. It was like arguing with a wall. Yes, he'd been hurt on the field, but he wasn't paralyzed. He could take care of himself. "I won't. I'll be careful—I promise."

Her bottom lip jutted out. "I'm just trying to take care of my baby brother. If someone's not here while I'm gone, I'll be sick with worry."

Oh, for the love…"Kim, I'll be fine."

She sniffed. "I'm going on my honeymoon, and all I'll be able to think about is you instead of William."

Seriously, she should've been an actress. "Cut that out."

"I'm being completely real here. You were in so much pain those first few months. I don't want to see you go through that again." Pouty lips and now doe eyes? Geez.

Completely real? How about completely manipulative. "I won't. Please don't hire a nurse, okay? I'll be extra careful. I'll actually get some alone time."

Her face fell, and her bottom lip trembled harder. Now he'd done it. "You mean you haven't wanted me here? All this time, you were wishing you were alone?"

Were those real tears he was seeing? Man, his sister was good. "No, that's not what I'm saying. I'm just…I was looking forward to just being here by myself. I can roll around in my underwear if I want. I can eat things you hate. That kind of thing."

"That's not how it sounded."

He groaned. "Wanting to be alone doesn't mean I haven't loved having you here. It means…"

"What?"

That he wanted to be alone. He could walk around without sneaking. Not have to worry about everything he did because his big sister was watching. "It means I want a moment to myself." He was tired of her constant hovering. He couldn't fix a sandwich without her asking if he needed help.

"And that's fine, but you can't be here two weeks by yourself with me out of the country. If you hurt your hip again, your career could be over. Do you want that?" His sister sank into the couch across from him.

Football was more than a career. It was his first love. Did he want it to be over? No, but the deeper reasons he was still in the wheelchair were ones he didn't want to talk about with his sister, or anyone else for that matter. "No, I love football."

"Okay, then that settles the argument. I'm hiring a nurse for at least two weeks."

His eyes widened. *At least* two weeks? "What does that mean?"

Kimberly looked at him like he was as dumb as a post. "I'm moving in with my husband. I won't be able to stay here anymore. You'll need someone here at least part-time."

"No, no, no. Nope. No way. I will be fine."

One lone eyebrow slowly went up. "Liam Jackson Thomas, I'm hiring a nurse, and if she's good, she'll be part-time until your hip is completely healed. I'm not taking any more lip from you. You got it?"

When did she become his mother? "I'm thirty-two years old! I don't need you to mother me!"

She flinched like he'd hit her.

He hung his head. He was dead.

"You're right. I don't," she said. "But I've been taking care of you since they died. It's been you and me for twenty years." The little exhale of breath was a knife. He'd hurt her without meaning to. "I'm sorry I'm trying to look out for you. It's become a habit. But don't worry. I'll leave you alone since I'm not your mother." She stood.

He wheeled to her and grabbed her hand. "I'm sorry, Kim."

"Yeah, you always say that."

"No, really, I am. It's just that it feels like you aren't listening to me. I want a moment to be in my house, by myself, and you're taking it like I'm doing it to hurt you." Liam looked up at her. Now it was his turn to try the weepy look.

"You need a nurse."

"No, I don't."

Kim's eyebrows knitted together. "Why can't you let me have this? I'm going on my honeymoon. If I go, leaving you here alone, I won't be able to do anything but worry. That's not how I want to spend my time if you get my drift."

He got it and wished he could bleach his mind. Either he was going to give in, or he was going to break her heart. Which was worse? "Okay, fine, but I don't have to like it. I'm not going to play nice."

"Then I'll just have to get a nurse who won't put up with it." In a blink, the tears were gone, and it was like she'd never been upset. She smiled and bent down to kiss his cheek.

His jaw dropped. "You are such a—"

"Watch your language. I'll start interviewing this week." She practically pranced away.

Liam held his head in his hands. His sister was a pain in the rear. Yeah, she loved him, but she loved him a little too much. There would be no nurse. He'd make sure of that. He'd behave as badly as he needed to ensure it.

THE BLUE GOOSE rolled to a stop in front of the large lodge home. Sara Lynch's 70s Pontiac boat of a Bonneville sounded like it sighed in relief as she cut the engine. The hill up to the home was nearly a straight climb, and Goosey had protested the entire way. Someday, Sara was going to get her restored to her original beauty, just like her dad had wanted.

Her phone rang in the seat next to her, and she squeezed her eyes shut. If she didn't answer, her mom would only keep calling. Picking up the phone, she took a deep breath and answered. "Hello, Mom."

"Hi, darlin'." Her mom giggled. Great. She was already drunk, and it was only eleven in the morning.

Why was she calling? Her mom knew she had an interview today. "What do you need, Mom?"

"I'm bored. I think I might try to find me another big fish."

She meant a male target. "Please, not while you're staying with me."

"I won't drag you into it."

If her mother happened to find a man dumb enough to fall for her and marry her, it'd make husband number five within three years. She would find a man with money, show interest in him, and then take him for all he had. Once all his money was gone, she'd then move, change her name, and start all over. This last time, she'd come to stay with Sara, promising not to run any con jobs while she stayed with her.

So far, Sara had managed to keep herself distanced from her mom's lifestyle. Once she figured out what her mom was doing, she didn't ask questions because she didn't want to know. She should be calling the police, but it was her mom. For some stupid reason, she just couldn't do it.

"You doing your scam in Denver? Is that smart?" Sara took a deep breath. Great. "You've already got a felony record for fraud. One more time and you're looking at prison. Why don't you find someone you really love, settle down, and be happy?"

"It'll be fine. And at least I haven't wasted six months of my life with a guy, only to have him dump me."

It was a low blow, and a lump formed in Sara's throat. He hadn't dumped her. The restraining order had dumped him.

Her mom continued. "I think if you crawled back, he might change his mind and take you back. Then you'd be taken care of too."

"I don't want a fish. Chris changed. He was mean and hateful. Don't you remember how bad he treated me?"

Her mom sucked her teeth. "Who cares? At least he had money."

"Yeah, he's got money and no soul. Winning the lottery brought out the worst in him. I'd rather find the poorest guy on the planet and have someone who really loves me than settle for a guy and his money."

"You do your thing; I'll do mine."

Why couldn't she have a normal mom? Why did she have to be a criminal?

"So, what *is* this new job?" her mom asked.

The client was private. All she knew was that he was thirty-two—four years older than her—and he had a hip injury. She'd had to sign a confidentiality agreement to even get the interview. "I don't have the job yet. It's just an interview today."

"With who?"

"They didn't say. The agency said when and where it was taking place and to be there on time." Which was now. "Hey, Mom, I need to go."

"Fine, fine. I know you don't like talking to me. I know you hate me. It's okay. I deserve your hate."

Her mom was the most manipulative person she'd ever met. "I don't hate you. My interview is in five minutes. I want to try to relax so I don't blow it."

"Then I guess I'll see you at the house later, huh?"

Unfortunately. "Yeah, I'll make dinner."

"That's my girl."

Hopefully, her binge effects would be worn off by then. "Bye."

Sara shook her head. She needed her mom out of her thoughts so she could concentrate on getting this job. For two weeks, she'd be staying at this fancy home and not dealing with her crazy alcoholic mother. If she had to catch a moonbeam with a fish net, she'd do it.

Leaning over in the seat, she let her gaze wander over the impressive home. It sure was gorgeous. Large front windows overlooking the mountain, rocking chairs sitting on the front porch, and not a neighbor for miles.

She couldn't help but wonder who could live in a such an incredible place. Whoever it was had great taste. If she ever made it big, after fixing Goosey, she'd be getting something like this and hiding for a few years. And she'd definitely keep her mom from finding out about it.

Looking down at her phone, she exhaled loudly. "Okay, girlfriend, get your net. You've got a moonbeam to catch."

CHAPTER 2

*K*imberly loomed over Liam in the living room. "I swear, you pull something like that again, and I will break your other hip. You got it?"

Not smiling was taking all his strength. "Pull what?"

"You like sponge baths?" She was nearly growling.

He shrugged. "Hey, if I'm getting a nurse, it may as well benefit me."

His sister pursed her lips. "You're being as malicious as you can so none of these nurses will want the job."

Yep. He didn't have Kim's trembling lip, but he did have an ornery streak. "Don't you want to know I'm in the best possible hands? I mean, if they see me at my worst now, they won't be quitting in the middle of the job."

The doorbell chimed, and Kim bent down. "You behave, or I'm going to take a picture of you naked and post it everywhere."

"No you won't." Although, the thought did strike a little fear in him.

She narrowed her eyes and pointed a finger at him as she walked to the door and opened it. "Hi, I'm Kimberly Thomas."

The next potential nurse stepped through the door, and for a second, Liam was stunned. None of the other nurses looked like her. Her light brown hair hung just below her shoulders in loose, long waves. She was maybe five and a half feet tall if she stood on her tiptoes, so not super short, but not exactly tall either. Under her long coat, he could see she wore a blouse and slacks.

Then she turned her gaze on him, and it was like a shock wave rolling through him. She had the most crystal Caribbean-green eyes he'd ever seen. So clear and green it was like they were made of glass.

"Hi, I'm Sara Lynch. I'm here for the interview."

Oh, right, nurse. He didn't care how green her eyes were, she wasn't staying. Not now, not ever.

Kimberly turned and squinted at him in warning

before waving for Sara to follow. "Let's sit over here in the living room. It's more comfortable."

"Sure," she said and followed his sister.

Kim took a seat in the armchair facing the wall of windows along the back of the house, and the woman sat on the couch closest to Kimberly as she removed her coat. Whoa. She was downright hot.

Liam wheeled himself into the living room behind them and parked. This was going to be easy and fun. He'd saved the best for last. "So, do you give sponge baths? The last nurse didn't."

"Don't mind him; he's being petulant." His sister pierced him with a look, picked up her phone, and lifted her eyebrows to remind him of her threat.

He didn't look half bad naked, and if it gave him alone time, it was worth it. "I had to ask."

Sara turned her gaze on him. "That depends. How cold do you like the water?"

Kimberly snorted. "Oh, I already like you." Reaching across to the coffee table, she grabbed a yellow file and flipped it open.

Liam looked away and muttered. Okay, not so easy. He was going to have to dig deep to rattle this chick.

"So, it says you've been an RN for eight years. You don't look old enough for that." Kimberly lifted her gaze from the file in her lap to Sara.

13

She smiled. "As soon as I graduated high school, I started working for my RN."

"What made you want to be a nurse?"

Liam looked at Sara, and for a brief second, he saw something flash in her eyes. Whatever. He still didn't need a nurse, and he didn't care about the answer.

"When I was seven, my dad was diagnosed with cancer. It had already spread to his lymph nodes and organs. Shortly after, he was put on hospice. The nurse who helped us was really nice, and I wanted to do that for others."

Really? Even Liam had a lump in his throat.

"Wow, uh, is that what you did, then? Work with hospice patients?" Kim asked.

She nodded. "Yeah, it's what I was doing until about two months ago."

"What made you decide to do something different?"

Liam looked away, pretending not to care about the answer. It's not like it mattered, he was not having anyone stay with him.

With a long, deep breath, she looked down at her hands. "My last hospice patient lived longer than most of my others. We got really close, and losing her was like losing a family member. I just need a little break so I can give the next family my best."

Kimberly reached out and touched her hand. "I can understand that. I'm sorry, though."

Sara looked up and smiled. "Thanks."

"So, have you always lived in Colorado?"

Her hair bounced as she shook her head. "No, I lived in South Carolina until I was eight. We moved right after my dad died."

"Oh, okay. A Southern Belle."

"No, just Southern."

Okay, this woman was well on her way to becoming nurse of the year, and his sister looked positively taken. He needed to do something and quick. "Do you cook? Because it's hard for me to cook."

"Yes, I can." Her lips spread into a smile that only added to her attractiveness.

For a second, his tongue was so tied he couldn't speak. He cleared his throat. "How about dry cleaning?"

"You're in jeans and a flannel button-up. Exactly how much dry cleaning could you have?"

Kim laughed.

Oh, he was so not done. "How about making the beds?"

"Can I do it while you're in it? It might improve your attitude."

He clenched his jaw. "If I'm your boss, you will not be allowed to talk to me like that."

"And if you're my boss and you think you're going to treat me like a maid, you're wrong." She sat up straighter and pulled her shoulders back.

Liam grumbled. "No, she's rude and obnoxious. I won't have it."

She trained those dazzling green eyes on him and said, "I'm good at my job, and I'm a perfect fit for this position. If you think this little tantrum is the worst I've dealt with, you're sadly mistaken. And, a little secret between the three of us, I know how to mix medication. I'll have you thinking you're wearing a pink tutu and dancing on a tabletop if you don't mind your manners."

His sister cackled. "You're hired."

"No, she's not." He looked at Sara. "No, you're not."

Kim touched her knee. "Don't listen to him. It's my decision, and you start in a week."

"You are not hiring her," Liam said.

"Baby brother, you've met your match, and she's hired. You might as well get on the train." Kimberly stood. "Let me take you on a tour."

SARA HAD no idea who this guy was, but he was a complete jerk. If she didn't need the break from her mom so bad, she'd have told them to stuff it and then left. Even after his sister laughed at her cold-bath joke, Sara was surprised Kimberly considered hiring her after she'd talked to him like that, but she couldn't just sit there and take his attitude. Sponge bath? Really? They'd see how he liked a sponge bath as she wheeled him over the cliff.

Even if he was cute, she wasn't giving him a bath. Dark red hair that touched his collar, close-trimmed beard, blue eyes, and a smattering of freckles covering his face made him mouthwatering gorgeous. His voice was incredible, deep and warm. It gave her goosebumps. He was massive too. If she had to guess, he was at least six feet tall, if not more, and as big as a house. The guy obviously worked out, a lot.

She rolled her eyes as she followed his sister out of the living room. The best thing for her was to picture him as a troll living under a bridge. He needed a nurse, and that's all he was getting. "This home is...incredible. I sat in the car and admired it before I knocked on the door."

"Yeah, I've loved living here. Liam got it about a year ago, right after he hurt his hip." Kimberly glanced at her. "Do you know who my brother is?"

She wanted to say, "A royal pain in your derriere?" But she didn't want to be rude, and the jerk was following behind them. Instead, she said, "No. I have no idea."

He cleared his throat. "Liam Thomas, the football player and billionaire."

A football star, huh? Well, that explained his size. Sara looked over her shoulder. "And that's supposed to mean something to me? I don't watch football and care even less about money." The money part put the brakes on any thoughts of him being attractive. Money ruined everything.

"See, now she's just being rude and nasty. She's not hired."

Two weeks without her mom. That was the goal. Sara turned around, put her hands on his wheelchair arms, and looked him in the eyes. "I've been around long enough to know what you're trying to do. I want this job, and I'll be here in a week. If your attitude hasn't changed by the time I get here, I'll show you what a real tackle looks like. Got it?"

His jaw dropped. "Um."

"Good boy." She pushed off the wheelchair and smiled, trying to ignore how great he smelled.

His sister bounced and laughed. "Oh, I love you. You are so very hired." She clasped her hands together.

"Now, this *is* a two-story home, but we primarily use the first floor. Liam had it modified to accommodate his wheelchair. He can go to the second floor with the chairlift, but like I said, we mostly stick to this floor."

"Okay," Sara said as she looked around.

Kimberly touched her arm, pulling her to a stop. "Oh, before I forget. I hate to do it because I really like you, but you'll need to sign a second confidentiality agreement. We can't have the press getting any information we don't want them to have. Is that a problem?"

"No," she said and glanced behind her at Liam. "No one should have to deal with that kind of pressure." Sara didn't have the press hounding her, but she did have a mother who made her feel trapped.

He glared at her with thin pinched lips. Boy, he sure didn't want her hired, but by the sounds of it, he didn't want anyone hired. She wondered why. Maybe she'd have a look at his medical records.

From what she understood, he had a hip injury, but it happened a year ago. It should have been healed already; with physical therapy, he should have been up and walking just fine.

She wondered why he'd still be pretending to be hurt if he wasn't. Maybe she needed to see life from his perspective: always expected to be great, with the press hounding him. Was there a chance he was scared to play football again?

Exactly how had he received the injury? That would probably give her more insight into him than anything. If it was bad, there was definitely a possibility of post-traumatic stress. It could happen to anyone, and it was nothing to be ashamed of.

Perhaps he needed more than a nurse. Maybe he needed a friend. She *was* going to be living there, and her job was to take care of him. It wasn't restricted to the physical.

"Sara?"

"Oh, sorry. I was just in awe of how beautiful this place is." Not a lie; she was. She took another quick glance at Liam.

One week to prepare. He was going to give her grief and try to make her quit. She knew that without a doubt, especially with the way he was grumbling. Years of living with her mom's abuse made Liam's attitude a cakewalk. It was almost funny.

"I do not want a nurse, and even if I did, I wouldn't want her," he said as he stared her down.

Oh yeah, he was going to be a real pill. Sara smiled. "I might not have the red hair, but I'm just as stubborn." She winked, and again his jaw dropped.

He muttered something as he turned his wheelchair around and rolled away.

"Nice meeting you," she called as she tiptoed.

Kimberly's wide eyes and a smile greeted her as she turned around. "Thank you."

"I'll stay here and take care of him. I promise." And she would, too. With or without his help.

CHAPTER 3

*S*tanding on the porch of Liam Thomas's home, Sara let her gaze roam over the panoramic painting-like scenery before her. So, this was what a billionaire view looked like. The guy sure knew how to pick a location. The air was so crisp and clean it was like water for her lungs.

She'd spent the last week preparing for the job, knowing full well he'd test every ounce of her patience. The final push she needed was her mom calling her at three in the morning, drunk and asking for a ride. For the next two weeks, her mother would have to take care of herself. As Sara rang the doorbell, she sent up a silent prayer that she'd leave her alone for once.

"I don't want a nurse," Liam called through the door. "Go home."

"Then I guess it's a good thing Kimberly gave me a key."

The door pulled open so fast the whoosh of air made her hair move. "My sister gave you a key?"

She quickly stepped inside and smiled. "No, but you opened the door, didn't you?"

Whoa, could this guy glower. It was incredibly cute. "I don't want you here."

"Then it's a good thing I don't work for just you. I promised your sister I'd take care of you so she could enjoy her honeymoon, and that's exactly what I'm going to do." Without another word, Sara walked around him and stopped in the middle of the living room. "This house is beautiful and large, but not so large you can get lost. I really like it."

"What do I have to do to get you to leave?" he said through clenched teeth.

She shrugged. "I guess you could stand up."

He threw up his hands. "You're as bad as she is."

"If you mean she cares about you, then yes, I am." She softened her posture. "I know you don't want me here, but I am. So why don't we try to make the best of the situation."

"Fine, but I have some rules." He wheeled toward her.

It took work not to roll her eyes. Rules? This would be interesting.

"You'll call me Mr. Thomas. If you're an employee, then I'm treating you like one." He was trying to hide his little smile, but she could see it. He was just being difficult.

"Okay."

A long pause.

"Is there more?" she asked.

"Yes. I just don't know what they are yet."

She pulled her lips in to keep from laughing. "Okay."

"Are you laughing?"

"No." But she sure wanted to.

Liam shook his head and looked away. "I wish she'd leave me alone. I wish you'd leave me alone. Why can't anyone listen?"

"Perhaps you are the one who isn't listening."

He jerked his attention back to her. "What?"

"Your sister loves you. She's lived with you for how long?"

"Not that it's any of your business," he crossed his arms over his chest, "but it's been about five years."

Sara nodded. "For five years, she's had peace of

mind, knowing you were being taken care of, especially since you had your injury. This is a love letter to you. It's her way of saying she's not abandoning you or picking her new husband over you."

"I know that."

"Did you ever think to tell her?"

His lips curved down. "Well…no."

"She was going out of the country, and you live on the side of a mountain. If anything happened to you while she was gone, she'd blame herself forever. This situation isn't all about you. It's about her knowing you're safe while she's gone."

"I told her I'd be fine."

"Yes, I'm sure you did, but how many times have you said that and you weren't?" She lifted her eyebrows and waited for an answer.

He took a deep breath. "I still don't want you here."

"I know, but lucky for you, your sister loves you enough to take care of you, despite your big-bad-wolf routine." Sara turned and walked down the hall to the bedroom Kim had shown her the week before.

About halfway down on the right, she entered the spacious room. Since seeing it the first time, she'd had dreams of staying in it. It had a sitting area and its own private bathroom. It was nicer than anywhere she'd stayed before. Definitely better than the two-bedroom apartment she shared with her mom. Not that she'd wanted to share, but she couldn't leave her mom out on the streets.

The four-poster bed was huge. It beat her twin any day. She crossed the room and set her luggage on top. It smelled so clean, as opposed to the alcohol stench she was used to. The room was simply incredible.

"I really don't want you here," Liam said.

Sara jumped and turned, pressing her hand to her chest. "Yes, I know."

"Then go home." The words came out like a growl.

She clasped her hands in front of her. "I'm sorry. I can't. I promised your sister I'd take of you, and I keep my promises."

He clenched his jaw. "I promise I'm going to make you regret being here."

"Mr. Thomas, there is nothing you can do to me that I haven't already dealt with. Now, if you want to see me as an enemy, that's your choice." She held her head high as she walked toward him. "I'm here for the next two weeks. I would like it if we could get along."

"Unfortunately for you, I don't want to get along. I want to be left alone." He spun his wheelchair around and rolled away.

Sara stepped into the hall and said, "It was lovely chatting with you."

Liam was so angry. She had to wonder if his sister wasn't seeing just how frustrated and lonely he was. He was used to being independent, and for the last year, he'd been trapped in a wheelchair.

SLAMMING THE DOOR, Liam parked his wheelchair, stood, and paced his room. He had to get that woman out of his hair. He'd spent the last year looking forward to Kimberly's honeymoon so he could have a moment's peace.

For once, he wished she would listen. Why couldn't she stop talking long enough to hear him? Were all women like that? So far, in his experience, the answer was yes. This Sara chick was just as bad.

It was lovely chatting with you? His whole body pulsated with anger.

So what if she was right? It didn't mean he had to like her. How could she keep her composure like that? Every other nurse, he'd rattled the second they stepped in the door. Not her.

He still couldn't get the moment she'd bent down and got in his face out of his mind. Her peppermint breath had mixed with whatever shampoo she'd used, and it made him dizzy—in a bad way, or so he kept telling himself.

There had to be a way to get rid of her. Something that would make her storm off and give him some peace. He wasn't trying to be a bad guy; he just wanted some space. Why couldn't Kimberly listen to him?

What could he do? Despite what she said, there had to be something that would drive her away. He just had to figure out what it was and then double it for good measure.

She didn't want to do sponge baths, and he wasn't keen on that himself. The idea of being a maid didn't appeal to her. He could tell by the way she'd reacted to the cooking and dry cleaning questions.

Yeah, if he treated her like a maid, she'd be out the door so fast she'd create a tornado. And he'd be free of his sister and her. He sat down in the wheelchair and rolled himself into the living room.

Sara was sitting in one of the armchairs, reading. She looked up and smiled. He had to give it to her; she had a great smile. Her eyes were some of the most beautiful he'd ever seen. "Hello."

For a heartbeat, his tongue was paralyzed. He didn't have time for any of that nonsense. She had to go. "I actually do have some dry cleaning I need taken in."

"Okay."

Wait. What? "You don't do dry cleaning." How could his plan be falling apart already?

She tilted her head. "And you don't have any dry cleaning. But if you'd like me to take your clean clothes and get them pressed, I'll be happy to. Is that all?"

"No. I expect you to cook. It's hard for me to do it, and since you don't mind dry cleaning, clearly cooking isn't beneath you either." He was even more frustrated now.

Her gaze locked with his and held it. He almost gulped. "If you would like me to cook for you, I'll be happy to. If you'll give me a list of your dietary needs and a schedule of when you'd like your meals, I'll make sure they're prepared as requested."

He groaned. "I want you to leave."

"What's made you so angry?"

"You," he snapped. It wasn't true. It wasn't her fault Kimberly was deaf.

"Well, we both know that's not true."

He jerked his gaze to hers. What? Was she a mind reader?

Her lips spread into a smile. "It's okay to be angry with the people we love, especially when we think they aren't hearing us."

"Then leave. Please, just leave." He didn't care if it sounded like begging. Desperate times called for desperate measures.

She bowed her head. "Had I realized what was going on when your sister hired me, I would've never promised her to take care of you. Now that I have, I can't leave. She put her trust in me, and that means something to me. It's clear she adores you."

"I know she loves me. I just want her to do it from afar." His shoulders sagged.

Sara stood and crossed the room, stopping in front of him. She bent down until she was eye level and held his gaze. It felt like the little jewels were boring into him. "Sometimes, the people who love us tend to love us the way they want to be loved, thinking everyone wants that type of love. It never occurs to them that the love someone is desperate for is completely different from what they're giving."

He leaned back. His tongue felt numb. "Uh."

"Did you want me to cook for you? Or were you just wanting to drive me away?" she asked as she straightened.

Oh, she *was* good. "I do want you to cook."

"All right. When would you like lunch?" She was so calm.

"I don't know. When I get hungry." He pursed his lips and looked at the floor.

She took a deep breath. "Mr. Thomas."

He looked up, and again her gaze captured his. "What?" The question came out as harsh as he could make it.

She bent down again, and his breath caught. For some reason, it felt like she was really seeing him. Her fingers threaded through his hair. There wasn't even a hint it was romantic. It felt innocent, like she was trying to comfort him. "Do you really want me to cook for you?"

"No." Was he really pulling a Kimberly pout?

A smile so sweet it nearly dripped sugar played on her lips. "I will leave you alone. I will cook your meals if you decide you'd like me to, but other than that, you won't know I'm here."

"You'll be breaking your promise."

She shook her head. "No, I won't. Sometimes taking care of someone is giving them the space to decide they want to be taken care of." Without another word, she straightened, walked out of the living room, and he heard the door down the hall shut.

CHAPTER 4

The next morning, Liam groaned as he wheeled himself into the living room. Sara stood by the couch, smiling with her hands clasped in front of her. Kimberly must have told her about his doctor's appointment. Great.

"You don't have to drive me. I can drive myself," he said, unable to keep the frustration out of his voice.

Her eyebrows drew together. "I did say I'd stay out of the way, so I'll leave you to it. If you're saying you can drive because you don't want me driving, I can call you a cab."

"You'd really let me go on my own?"

She smiled. "Unless you think you'll perish, in which case I'll need to accompany you so I can go down with the ship."

He looked away but couldn't keep the smile off his face. She was incredibly witty and likable. It was just... he couldn't let himself like her. She needed to go, and the only way that was going to happen was if he had the chance to be so unbearable that she'd be left with no choice but to leave. Maybe his appointment would prove a good opportunity to chase her off. If he had to be nasty, then that's what he'd be. Space was calling him, and he felt compelled to answer. "No, you can drive."

She shrugged. "Okay, are we taking your car or mine?"

He looked at her. "Uh, I don't know if I trust you to drive my car. What do you have?"

She didn't even bat an eye while answering him. "A 1977 Pontiac Bonneville. Her name is Goosey."

Yeah, no. "I think we'll take my car."

She smiled. "Okay. Lead the way."

If he was honest, her smile was the warmest he'd seen in a long time. He shook his head to clear the thought. That was the last thing he needed to be thinking about.

He wheeled himself through the kitchen and mudroom and stopped in the garage. This was his favorite part of the house. He'd added on to the garage so it'd house at least six cars. It only had four at the moment, but when, or if, he was back on the field, he was planning on celebrating by buying another car.

Sara's gaze roamed over the room. "Wow, the garage is as nice as the inside of the house."

He rolled his eyes. "Of course it is. I'm a guy."

"Right. Well, which of these would you like to take?" Still calm and collected.

It was driving him nuts. What he wouldn't give to see her rattled. Just a little. "We'll take the Mercedes. And please be careful. It's a $300,000 one-of-a-kind AMG." He held up the keys.

"I have no intentions of being anything but careful." Her slender fingers wrapped around the keys, and she pulled them out of his hand.

A zing shot through him, and he jerked his hand back. Whatever. Not happening. Next subject. Still not rattled, even when he was being completely awful? What would it take?

Once he was in the car and his wheelchair was in the trunk, she got in and started the engine. "This is a really nice SUV. Are the seats Napa leather?"

"Yeah, how'd you know?" Most women didn't even notice the seats.

She waved him off. "Just something I read on the internet."

He plugged the address into the navigation system. "We can go now. Just follow the directions."

The garage opened, and she eased the vehicle out of the garage and started down the mountain. Liam looked over his shoulder and scoffed. "That's your car? It's awful." It was a land yacht, a big blue boat. It looked like it was barely held together. He wasn't even sure how it made it up the mountain.

"Yes, in its current state it is." Her tone never wavered, and she kept her eyes forward.

"Why don't you wear scrubs like a normal nurse?" he asked, his tone clipped. Even if he was genuinely curious, she didn't need to know that.

She shrugged. "I don't know. The agency I work for gave me an option, and I'm comfortable in a shirt and slacks."

A phone began ringing, and he looked at her purse sitting between them. He hated to do it, but if this was his chance to get rid of her, he had to take it. "A phone call? While on the job?" He snatched it off the top. This would have to shake her up a little. "And from your mom? How cute." Yeah, this would get her to stepping, no doubt.

She quickly glanced at him. "Please don't answer that. I'll call her back while you're in with the doctor." There was a tiny crack in her voice.

This was it. He answered the call and put it on speaker. "Hello?"

"Who is this?" The woman's words were slurred slightly, like she might be drunk.

Oh no. He'd made a huge mistake. "Uh, I'm just answering for your daughter so you don't worry. She'll call you in about twenty minutes." He squeezed his eyes shut and mentally thumped himself.

He heard something crash, and then her mom said, "You tell that lousy, no good, rotten daughter that she didn't leave me enough money for food."

"I'll be sure to give her the message." Liam quickly hung up the phone.

Sara swallowed hard and took a deep breath. "Thank you for answering that. At least now she won't worry."

Liam raked his hand through his hair. He was such a jerk. Why had he done that? "I'm so sorry. I only want to make you leave."

She straightened her shoulders. "I promised your sister I'd take care of you, and I keep my promises."

"You've never broken one?" Everyone broke their promises.

She nodded. "Once."

"Oh, have you? Care to share?" He grinned, waiting for the usual answers. I promised my high school boyfriend I'd love him forever. I promised I'd take care of my pet goldfish.

"I promised my dad I wouldn't cry when he died."

He closed his eyes and massaged his temple. Geez. It was like a butcher knife to the heart. What could he say? I'm a giant jerk? "I'm really sorry."

"Yeah." Her response was so soft he almost didn't hear it.

"You lost him when you were eight, right?" he asked. He was genuinely curious, and he hoped it showed.

She nodded. "Yes. I turned eight that day."

He died on her birthday? His head dropped on the back of the seat. Now, all he had to do was go out and find a puppy to kick. "Sara, I owe you an apology. I wanted to have some space. I wasn't—"

"I know, and I've handled worse." She sure seemed able to get herself together quickly. He wasn't sure he would have handled his behavior half as well.

Glancing at her, he nodded. "Yeah, I get the feeling you have." There were jerks, and then there was him. Once his visit was over and they were driving back, he'd talk to her again. He'd offer a truce and apologize as profusely as he knew how.

WHEN SHE GOT the early morning notice about Liam's doctor's appointment, she expected something more doctorly. The home she was stopping in front of looked less like a doctor's office and more like a residence.

Sara eyed the large home. "This doesn't look like a doctor's office." It had two stories, stone and brick, and she guessed it was well over ten thousand square feet. It more than dwarfed Liam's home.

"Yeah, I know. It's my friend's house. I put it in as a doctor's appointment because it's for mental health." He smiled.

She nodded. "Okay. I'll be here when you're done."

"You're just going to sit out here and wait? You don't want to come in?"

"No, I'll stay out here. Take as long as you want." She got out of the SUV and brought his wheelchair around, holding it while he settled himself in. "Is there anything you'd like me to do while you're visiting?"

He shook his head. "No, but you really don't have to stay in the car."

"I'll be here when you're done." She smiled and walked around the car to get back in her seat.

"Okay. I won't take too long," he said and wheeled away.

With Liam gone, Sara took her phone out and

dialed her mom. Maybe she'd be lucky and her mom wouldn't have had any more to drink since Liam answered the phone.

"Hello?"

Sara's shoulder's sagged. "Hey, Mom." No such luck. She was even tipsier than before, and it wasn't even noon yet. How was her mom able to pull con jobs with as much as she drank?

"You rotten, hateful thing. You didn't leave me any money at all." Her tone was shrill.

"Did you look in the freezer?" She'd stuck it in there so her mom wouldn't spend everything all at once.

"Now why would I look in there, idiot?"

Sara gritted her teeth. "I've asked you not to talk to me like that."

"Don't you get snippy with me, you nasty thing. I bet you're lying, thinking I'll buy anything."

"I'll wait while you look."

After a bunch of cursing and some shuffling, there was a sound of a door swishing open. "Oh, I guess you did leave money."

"I told you I did."

"I'm sorry, sweetheart. I was just cranky. I didn't mean any of it. I love you, and you're such a great daughter for always taking care of me."

Just before she hit the wasted stage, she was a blend of manipulation, sweet, and mean. It was a minefield to know which one it would be every time her mom opened her mouth.

If it was anyone other than her mom, she'd have already put her out on the streets. She wasn't sure why she put up with it, anyway. Calling Regina "Mom" was a joke. But she still couldn't muster the courage to cut her off. She was an enabler, and she hated that she was.

"Did you pay the rent before you left?"

"Yes, I did. Why do you ask?"

"I'm tired of living here. I want to move somewhere else."

Sara rolled her eyes. Not this again. "It's what I can afford."

"Not if you'd stayed with Chris."

"He hurt me, Mom, remember?" Her ex had won the lottery six months before they broke up. The money changed him. It was like night and day. The man she'd loved had been replaced with a prima donna jerk. The last straw was when he attacked her.

"So? He had money. We could be living anywhere we want. Twenty million isn't anything to sneeze at, you know?"

"I didn't want his money."

Like the pop of a top, mean mom was about to be unleashed. "You're so stupid. You could have taken a little off the top and squirreled it away, and then you would've had something."

"That's fraud, Mom. I'd lose my RN license."

"With money, you wouldn't need it."

"I like my job." And she got a break from her mom.

Liam wasn't nearly as bad as her mom. She'd pick his little tantrums over her any day. At least he was good-looking. Not that she thought of him that way. So what if little butterflies had started flitting when he was around? It didn't matter. He was a client.

Sara shook her head to clear her thoughts and leaned her forehead against the steering wheel. She closed her eyes, silently praying her mom would get caught before her job with Liam was over. What would life be like without the constant stress her mother brought?

"You like your job or you like your *client*?"

"I love my job. My clients are not dating material." Even if he was drop-dead gorgeous.

"Well, you just keep loving your job. See how well it loves you back."

It gave her fulfillment. "Is there anything else you need?"

"Is there any more money in the house?"

Yes, but she wasn't going to tell her that. If she did, her mom would be calling and demanding more. "No, I left all I had."

"I guess I'll hit up my new fiancé." She laughed.

"Okay, Mom. I'll talk to you later."

No bye, nothing. Just a silent phone.

Everything would be okay. If her mom got caught again, then it was on her. Sara did wonder what her dad would say if he was still alive. Would he be proud of who his daughter had become? What would he think of the promise she made to take care of her mom? Would he still want her to keep her promise if he knew how horrible Regina was?

It had taken every bit of her strength to hold it together when Liam asked about him. Her dad didn't like to see her cry, and he didn't want her to mourn him. He wanted her to be happy for the time they had together. It was her only broken promise, ever.

Another twelve days without her mom. That's all she needed to remember. No alcohol, no verbal berating—or at least not as much—and no mother. Fresh, clean air and a clean house and room. It was like getting paid to be on a vacation.

Sara yawned. She was running out of steam. If she leaned the seat back, maybe she could catch a nap before Liam came out. With a little sleep under her belt, she could continue to keep herself composed.

The seat leaned back so quietly that if she hadn't been moving, she would swear it wasn't working. The leather was buttery soft, and the seat was almost as cushiony as a bed. But honestly, with as weary as she felt, she could've probably slept on a bed of rocks. It really was a nice car. One she'd never be able to afford. But she loved Goosey, and one day she'd be just as comfortable.

Visions of the old car made shiny and new swam before her as she drifted off without even realizing it.

CHAPTER 5

*L*iam opened the door of the SUV, and Sara popped up.

"Sleeping on the job, huh?" he asked.

"Yes, I guess I was." She got out of the car and held his wheelchair while he got in. She stowed it in the back and then got back in.

"How do you do that?" His eyebrows were furrowed as he looked at her.

She tilted her head. "How do I do what?"

"Keep your cool. It's like nothing rattles you. It's… infuriating," he said as he shut his door.

Her gaze traveled down to her hands in her lap. "I don't know."

"Well, stop it. Show some emotion or something. It's like dealing with a robot." He shook his head and

45

turned his attention out the window. What was his damage? It wasn't even like she was hovering. She'd actually been rather nonexistent.

Sara started the car. "Is there anywhere else you'd like to go while we're in town?"

Without looking at her, he said, "No."

"Okay."

He'd promised himself he'd apologize, and he'd started the return ride with being a jerk again. What was his deal? Why was she making him so crazy? "I'm sorry about earlier...and just now. If you'd like, we could get lunch or something as a way to make it up to you."

"I accept your apology, but you don't need to take me to lunch. If *you'd* like to stop, I'd be happy to take you somewhere." She kept her eyes on the road as she spoke.

There was Robot Sara again. How was he going to make it another twelve days with her like that? Avoiding her wasn't working. He actually found himself liking her. She was cute and funny. Wait. What? No, he didn't. He liked it that she kept to herself. The last thing he needed was a meddling woman *or* nurse.

He was hungry, though, and lunch did sound pretty good. "There's a little burger place not far from here. Would you at least have a burger with me?"

She glanced at him, and it looked like she was debating. "That would be nice; thank you."

It had to stop being so weird. "Look, how about a truce? I will stop being a jerk if you'll relax and be less robot-like."

"I'll agree on one condition."

Oh great. "What's that?"

"If you need help, you promise to ask. Please don't re-injure your hip. Your sister loves you, and I promised to take care of you." She glanced at him. "Please."

Man, this woman knew how to lather it. "If that will keep you out of my hair, then fine."

"Then I agree."

"Thank you." He felt like he could breathe again. "I just wanted some space. I didn't want to hurt Kimberly. I know she loves me, but I feel like I'm being smothered."

"I can see that."

He snuck a glance at her. "Could you do me another favor?"

"What's that?"

"Could you stop being so composed? It's unnerving. Just be yourself, okay? Remember, we have a truce." He didn't need her life story or her friendship, but this—whatever it was—had to go.

Sara nodded. "I can try. This is me, or me at work, Mr. Thomas."

Mr. Thomas? Really? Yeah, he'd told her to call him Mr. Thomas, and she was at work. He wanted a professional distance, and that's what he was getting. "Okay."

"Could you point me to the restaurant you want to go to?" she asked.

Oh yeah, lunch. "Yeah, take a left at the next light, and it's about halfway down on the left. Greasy Burger."

They rode in silence the rest of the way, and she parked. He'd picked the place because they could order from the car.

"I've never been here before," Sara said as she looked around. "I've driven by it but never stopped."

He shrugged. "It's a serious hole-in-the-wall, but the food is delicious. I've never had a better burger, and the onion rings are out-of-this-world good."

"Is that what you'd like me to order for you?"

"And you. Your stomach growled." He chuckled.

Her cheeks turned a bright pink. She tucked a piece of hair behind her ear. "Uh, okay."

It was the first real emotion he'd gotten from her

that wasn't directed at him because he was a jerk. "Bacon cheeseburger, lettuce, tomato, onion, avocado, mustard, and mayo, with onion rings. Oh, and a root beer."

"They'll be able to smell your breath from Mars." She clamped her hands over her mouth and looked out the window as she chuckled.

He threw his head back and laughed. That was more like it. "If you get the same, we can get to Jupiter."

She rolled down the window and ordered two identical meals with drinks. When she was done, she rolled the window back up and fidgeted with her coat cuffs.

Silence stretched out until it became so uncomfortable that Liam squirmed. Finally, he said, "Thanks for having lunch with me." He touched her hand and then jerked his back. Whoa. He wasn't expecting that. The tingle from the small touch traveled up his arm, and he shivered.

Sara looked down as she nodded. "You're welcome." She turned her head toward him, and the longest lashes he'd ever seen fanned out against her cheeks. When she lifted her gaze, she was looking at him through those long lashes, and his pulse jumped.

Oh, she couldn't be doing that. "Uh, well…I, uh,

uh...oh look, our food is here." He sent up a silent prayer of thanks for the save. Good waiter. He was getting an excellent tip today.

She rolled down the window and took the food, and Liam paid. The smell was so good his mouth watered. He was hungrier than he thought.

"Yikes, this smells like it could be addictive." She gave a little laugh.

It was cute too. What? No, no cute laughs, no pretty eyes. And she couldn't be giving looks like the one he'd received earlier. And definitely no more tingly touches. She was...something...just not...something he was interested in. That's right. That was a no can do.

He ripped open the burger and took a giant bite. "Eat up," he said with a mouth full of food. The more disgusting he was, the better.

As he watched her, she peeled hers open and took a bite. He was pretty sure he heard her moan.

"This is so good. I guess I was pretty hungry." She closed her eyes and bowed her head. "Thank you for lunch."

"You're welcome. So, I was right?"

Sara caught her bottom lip between her teeth as she turned her green eyes on him and held his gaze. "Yes, thank you. I mean...thanks."

His heart galloped. Whoa there, buddy. He belched like he was getting paid for it. "Sorry." Not sorry. Disgusting, wallowing, muddy pig not sorry.

She chuckled. "If you're trying to gross me out, you'll have to do better than that. I've got stories that will curl your toes."

Her laugh was cute, and he liked hearing it. What was his problem? He should have stuck with the fifty-year-old male nurse. If he could go back, he'd have behaved and this beautiful woman wouldn't be here. Gah. He had to stop.

A TRUCE WITH LIAM. That could be interesting. Sara nibbled on her burger while Liam seemed to engulf his whole. She hadn't realized how hungry she was until she bit into it. It was so juicy and flavorful she'd literally moaned. She only hoped he hadn't heard it.

At least he wouldn't be behaving like a jerk anymore. He was really charming when he wanted to be. It added to his attractiveness...which she wasn't noticing because he was a client.

"The onion rings are fantastic, right?" he asked.

To die for, with just the right crunch. "Yes, the best I've ever had."

She looked up, and her heart dropped. Her mom was standing across the way. If she saw Sara, she'd know who she was working for. Sara pushed the food onto the seat and slipped down onto the floor.

"Um, what are you doing?" He was looking at her like she'd lost her mind.

She had. She'd never had to duck her mom before, but she couldn't find out about Liam. What could she tell him? She touched her forehead to the seat. "My mom is right over there. I don't want her to see me. If she does, then she'll know who I'm working for, and she can't know that."

"Your mom's here?"

"Yes, and I don't even know how. She was partially drunk when she called." Her voice broke. "Why did she have to be here?"

"It's okay. She's a little hammered. I've handled worse."

She rolled her head and looked at him. "It's not just that." It was getting harder to fight back tears. Liam didn't need to know about her mom or her problems. Knowing about her mom's drinking was bad enough.

"Then what?"

Lifting her head, she sighed. "She's a con artist. She finds men and then takes their money. She started doing it a few years ago. I don't know why. It was like one day she woke up and decided, 'Hey, I'll go be a thief.'"

"So, she wasn't always doing it?"

Talking about her mom was pushing her to her limit. "No, before that she was a gambler. She got caught cheating at a Vegas casino, and they banned her."

"Wow."

She squeezed her eyes shut and covered her mouth with her hand. Her endless well of composure seemed to find its end as tears trickled down her cheeks. "I'm so sorry. Is she gone yet?"

"I can't make out who she's riding with, but it looks like she's got her food and is getting ready to leave." He leaned down and touched her hand. "It's okay. You can't control who gave birth to you."

Sara looked at him. "She can't find out about you. She'll do anything for money. I don't know what she'd do to you, but she'd find something. I promised to take care of you. That promise included all of you—even your money." Her imagination ran wild with the things her mom would do to Liam. She couldn't let it happen.

He looked up, and when he looked back down at her, he smiled. "She's gone."

She collapsed against the seat. "Oh, thank goodness."

As she started to get up, he took her hands to help her. The shock of his touch made her hit her head, and she rubbed it as she sat down.

Liam grimaced. "I'm sorry. I was trying to help. Are you okay?"

"I'm okay. Thank you." She hung her head and wiped her eyes. Nothing like that had ever happened to her in her entire career. Why did it have to happen now? Liam was wealthy. He'd be the perfect target for her mom.

He leaned forward in the seat and turned her face toward him. "It's okay. You haven't done anything wrong. In fact, you're as close to perfect as I've ever seen. At least where nurses are concerned."

She chuckled.

"What?" he asked as he leaned back.

"I think you hit Jupiter on your own." She captured her bottom lip between her teeth and laughed a little louder.

He threw his head back, and his laugh was amazing. It was the second time she'd really heard him laugh, and she loved the throatiness of it. "You're something else."

"I'm sorry," she said, trying to rein in her laughter.

"No, I'm sorry, and I'm amending the truce."

She tilted her head. "What?"

He rubbed the back of his neck. "If I'm honest, I've liked having you around. You're witty, and I enjoy your company. I still don't want to be waited on, but I don't mind you being at the house."

The little freckle above his lip was almost winking at her. Boy, was he charming and easy to like. She just had to make sure the line in the sand she had for herself didn't get blurry. It wasn't hard to picture doing more than enjoying his laugh.

CHAPTER 6

*L*ate that night, Sara blinked awake and groggily grabbed her phone. She didn't know what woke her up, but at least it wasn't her mom. What *had* woken her up? She'd slept pretty well since she'd started working for Liam. The bed was comfortable, and it smelled so clean.

Throwing the covers off, she slid off the bed and went to the kitchen. It was late, so she wouldn't be running into him. Other than cooking his meals, she'd tried to steer clear of him by mostly staying in her room. They had a truce, but no matter what he said, he needed his space. She almost wanted to thank him. It was the first time in a while she'd be allowed to relax and catch up on her sleep.

She poured herself a glass of water and leaned her hip against the counter as she took a drink.

"What are you doing in here?" Liam asked as he flipped the lights on.

Her heart hammered as she jumped. The water sloshed out of the glass and down her shirt. He'd scared the daylights out of her. She set the glass down, grabbed a paper towel, and patted her shirt down. "I was thirsty. I'm sorry if I woke you. I was trying to be quiet." She pressed her hand against her chest and took a deep breath.

"You didn't. I couldn't sleep." His voice was off.

She narrowed her eyes. He didn't look right either. "Something's not right."

"What? No, nothing's wrong." He backed his chair up and hit the bar separating the kitchen from the living room.

Now that she was really looking at him, it wasn't only his voice. His cheeks were flushed. She walked to him and placed her hand on his forehead. "You're blistering hot."

He brushed her hand from his forehead. "I'm not. It's just from getting in and out of this wheelchair."

Right. He was terrified of letting his sister know she was right. Not that he couldn't handle a fever on his own, but it would solidify Kim's reasons to worry.

If that happened, he'd be so trapped he'd lose his mind. She couldn't blame him for trying to hide being sick.

Sara caught his gaze and held it. "I give you my solemn promise that if your sister calls, I will tell her you haven't needed me at all. That I'm so bored it is mind-numbing."

"You will?" He sounded like he felt terrible.

"She'll never know. It'll be our secret." Kimberly would never find out. At least not from her.

Liam's shoulders drooped. "I don't feel very good."

"Will you let me take care of you?"

He looked down and nodded. "I hate this. I didn't want her to be right." He lifted his gaze to hers, and Sara could see how hard the last year had been on him.

"She wasn't. You can take care of yourself. You're just sick and lucky enough to have a nurse living with you at the moment." She winked. "Let's get you back into bed, okay?"

Sara walked next to him as he wheeled himself back to his room. It wasn't as big as she thought it'd be. For a billionaire, it was actually modest. Well, the whole house was.

"It hurts my chest to lie flat," he said as he stopped by the bed.

"I'll be right back." She went back to her room and grabbed all the pillows she could carry. Back in his room, she placed the pillows so he'd be sitting up but still able to sleep comfortably. When she was finished, she turned and asked, "Do you need help getting out of the wheelchair?"

He rolled his eyes but nodded. "A little." Boy, he hated needing help. He wanted to be free again.

With a little work, she got him on the bed. She turned, and he grabbed her arm. "Are you leaving?"

His touch was making her heart race. He was sick, and there was no time for that. Even if he wasn't sick, she wasn't interested. "I'm going to get you some ice, a cold cloth for your head, and some water. Maybe I'll find a thermometer while I'm at it; otherwise, I'll have to resort to kissing your forehead." She smiled. "I'll be right back." When he didn't let go of her arm, she added, "I promise."

Liam released her, and she left the room.

While she gathered the things she needed, she wondered how long he'd been sick. He was so afraid of his sister finding out he'd needed someone that he was willing to suffer in silence rather than prove her right. Sara felt a prick of sympathy for him.

Kimberly needed to hear him and soon, or she would drive a wedge between them so far it would be hard to remove it. Love had a way of making people blind, and Kimberly was completely unaware of how much he resented her at the moment.

After she'd found everything, she returned to his room and sat beside him. She placed the cold cloth on his head, and he exhaled like it was a relief.

"Thank you," he said and looked at her.

She stuck the thermometer in his mouth and waited until it beeped. Almost a hundred and three. "You keep this fever up, and you'll be getting that cold-water sponge bath you wanted so badly."

His laugh was soft, and he grinned. "I just didn't want you here."

"I kinda got the message." She brushed her fingers across his cheek. "How long have you been sick?"

He looked down. "I didn't feel great when I woke up this morning, and I was feeling worse when I went to bed. I woke up a little while ago, sick to my stomach."

She shook her head and then narrowed her eyes. "You heard me in the kitchen and came out to see if I'd notice, didn't you?"

His eyebrows knitted together. "How do you do that?"

"I told you I'm very good at my job." She started to move, and he wrapped his fingers around her arm. Oh, hello, tingles. It was like she'd touched an electric fence.

He hesitated a second and then said, "Please don't go."

She held his gaze. "I'll stay as long as you want me to."

"Why are you being so nice to me?" He let his hand drop across his stomach. "I've been a complete jerk to you."

Sara leaned forward. "Despite your attitude, I like you."

Liam was quiet a moment as he seemed to gauge her answer. "Why?"

What could she say? "I've got no deep answer. There's just something about you." It was the absolute truth. For some unknown reason, she really liked him, and it bothered her a little. Butterflies would tickle when she was around him. That hadn't happened with a client before.

"Would you like some ice?"

He nodded.

After feeding him a few bites, she leaned forward and ran her fingers across his cheek again. "I wish you'd come to me sooner."

"You really care, don't you?"

With a nod, she said, "I really do. I hate that you're sick."

He held her gaze for a moment, and she wondered what he could possibly be thinking. "You're very pretty. You have the most beautiful eyes I've ever seen."

A chuckle popped out before she could stop it. That hadn't been on the list of things she thought he might be thinking. "You must be feeling awful."

"Doesn't change the fact that you're beautiful." He closed his eyes and took a deep breath. "I'm so tired."

She covered his hand with hers. "Rest. I'm not going anywhere."

Another deep breath, and he drifted to sleep. His cheeks were so red they almost matched his hair. He was sick, sick enough she was glad she was staying with him. She'd known he wasn't as boorish as he was pretending to be.

There was something about him that was drawing her to him. She shook her head. This was a job, and he was a client. Cupid needed to take a hike.

IT WAS a long night for Liam and an even longer day. He'd fallen asleep, only to be woken up with a sick stomach again. His head hurt, his chest hurt, and his whole body ached. He went from cold to hot to cold in a matter of minutes.

He hated that his sister was right, that he'd needed someone. But he was grateful for Sara. When she said she'd stay with him, she'd meant it. Not once did she leave his side during the night, even after all the grief he'd given her the previous couple of days.

"Hey," she said as she walked into his room. Her hair was wet, and she wore a clean set of pajamas. She covered her mouth as she yawned and sat beside him. "I needed a shower."

"You don't have to keep staying. I'm feeling better." He wanted her to stay, but not if she didn't want to.

Her smile was amazing. "Do you want me to stay?"

When she said she was good at her job, she wasn't kidding. She'd earned his respect in one night. "Not if you don't want to."

She looked down, and her eyebrows knitted together. Long eyelashes fanned out against her cheeks, and when she looked back up, even feeling as bad as he did, his breath caught. This look was the one that sent you to your knees. "I told you I wouldn't get in your way. I'll stay, but only if you still want me to."

It was a good thing she wasn't taking his pulse.

He'd be answering without speaking. "I...do. I mean, I would like that."

"Then I'll stay. I'll stay until you don't want me to." She leaned forward and touched his forehead. "How are you feeling?"

"Better." And it'd taken until sunset to get to that point.

Sara narrowed her eyes. "What's your definition of better?"

He chuckled. "Well, I don't want to be shot and put out of my misery."

"I'd say that's improvement. Are you hungry?"

"Not really." He let his head drop back on the pillow. She'd kept him propped up during the night, and it'd helped a lot.

Her phone starting ringing, and she pulled it out. "Talk about crazy timing. It's Kimberly," she said and answered the phone, putting it on speaker.

He thought for sure she'd step out of the room to speak to her, but she stayed right next to him.

She put her finger to her lips and smiled. "Hey, Kimberly. How's the honeymoon?"

"Amazing. I'm calling to make sure Liam is behaving himself."

Sara's eyes bored into his. "He's been fine."

His mouth dropped open. Why was she lying for

him? Even when she said she wouldn't tell, he hadn't believed her, not really. He'd been a complete and utter jerk. Why would she do that?

"Are you just trying to keep me from worrying?"

"Kimberly, you're on your honeymoon with your new husband. Why are you calling, really?" She continued to hold his gaze.

"I don't know. I worry about him."

Her eyebrows knitted together, and she looked down at the bed. "Do you mind if I speak freely?"

"Sure."

"I can't begin to imagine what it must have been like to see him get hurt. I bet that moment in time is seared into your memory."

His sister sniffed. "It still replays in my head. I practically raised him. When it happened, my heart stopped. I don't want him hurt again."

Liam hadn't even thought about what she must have gone through. He should have, but he'd been pretty wrapped up in himself the last year.

"I know, but have you considered that maybe, just maybe, you're being a little too loving?"

"What do you mean?"

"There are thousands of people permanently confined to a wheelchair, living their lives and fully capable of taking care of themselves. I know you love him, but you're smothering him. If you don't pull back a little, you're going to drive a wedge between the two of you, and I don't think you want that."

He was staring at Sara, stunned. How was she able to do that? To read a situation and know what was going on? Yeah, he'd told her a little, but Kimberly's motivations weren't something she would've known about.

"I didn't even think about that."

Sara kept her head down, and those long eyelashes were fanned out against her cheeks. "I know, which is why I'm mentioning it. I think he feels like he's being treated like a child. He's not. He's a grown man."

Another sniff. "I know you're right. I just..." A little sob echoed across the line.

"Love him." She drew circles on the bed with her finger as she spoke. "He's pretty likable when he's not being a bear, isn't he?"

"He's a wonderful man. He's kind, sweet, and caring. I wish he'd find someone real to love. Those models he's dated are not worth his time."

His sister thought that about him? She'd never said anything like that. Then again, when was the last time they'd really talked? Lately, it felt like he was talking and she was talking, but they weren't having a conversation as much as making noise.

When Sara spoke again, her voice was tender. "I admire your love and dedication. I've taken care of patients who I wished had someone like you taking care of them. You really are wonderful. I want you to know that."

He was in awe. She'd said all the things he'd wanted to say for the last year, and it actually sounded like Kim was listening.

Another little sob. "You really think so?"

"Absolutely." Sara paused. "Now, go enjoy your honeymoon, and don't worry about him. I promised you I'd take care of him, and I will. If anything happens to him, it'll be over my dead body."

"I'm so glad you're there. I promise I will stop worrying and enjoy my honeymoon." His sister laughed. "And, once I'm back, I'll sit down and talk to him. I promise I'll listen too."

Her lips curved up. "I'll hold you to that."

Sara ended the call and shook her head.

"How did you do that?"

She startled and looked up. "I'm so sorry. I got caught up in the conversation."

Without even thinking, he pulled her into a bear hug. "I don't know how to thank you."

"You could start by giving me oxygen."

He quickly let her go. Why did he do that? Why didn't he just say thanks? "I'm sorry. I've just…"

"Needed some space."

"Yeah."

She grinned. "I've been telling you I'm very good at my job."

Not good. Fantastic. If she'd managed to actually get his sister to back off, it would be a Christmas miracle. One he was ready for. Maybe if Kim stopped badgering him, it would give him a chance to figure out what was really eating at him. Maybe then he'd have enough courage to stand up again.

CHAPTER 7

Sara stretched and yawned as she opened her eyes. The sky was overcast, and she'd slept better than she had in months. Kimberly was going to get a hug from her. The bed was amazing.

A knock came from the door, and she threw the covers off. She'd hoped to take a shower and get dressed before leaving the room. With a one shoulder shrug, she opened the door. "Good morning," she said and smiled. Wait. Didn't he want to be left alone?

"Uh, yeah. Um, good morning." His eyes were wide like he'd been caught stealing gum from the grocery store.

She tilted her head. "Do you need some help? Are you feeling okay?"

"I'm okay," he said and rubbed the back of his neck.

"I thought since I was cooking breakfast, maybe you'd like some. I mean, if you're hungry." His lips spread into a little smile, and the freckle right above his top lip was like a beacon for her eyes. She needed to look at something else.

"Sure, that would be nice." She followed him down the hall and to the dining room table. It was quite the spread. Eggs, bacon, waffles. Who was he feeding, a small village? "Wow, this looks delicious and huge."

"Thanks. Have a seat. I'm starved."

She snorted. "Well, you won't be after this."

He chuckled. "I am a football player, you know."

"True. Have you missed playing football?"

His lips twitched. "Yeah, I have."

"But you aren't sure it's what you want to do anymore."

He jerked his gaze to hers. "What? Why would you say that?"

"The way your lips turned down as you said it." She pulled off a piece of bacon from the pile and nibbled it.

"That's not true." His tone wasn't quite harsh, but it was close to the one he used before they went to town.

The warning was clear. This was a touchy subject with him. Sara shrugged. "I've been wrong a lot in the past, so it wouldn't be the first time."

"Well, you are. I love football. The rush, the physical push to do more and be better...I've always loved it." He piled his plate with eggs, several slices of bacon, and several waffles. If he ate all of that, she would be truly impressed. "How about you? Do you play any sports?"

As if. "I typically don't have time."

He lifted an eyebrow. "Did you really not know who I was?"

"No. I'd never seen you before the interview. I couldn't have picked you out of a lineup." She laughed.

He chuckled and took a huge bite of his waffles. When he finished the bite, he said, "Well, I have an intense desire to stay away from lineups."

"Most people do." She wished her mother was counted among them. Her last jaunt to the county jail had almost landed her in prison, but the evidence had been messed up or something. Sara hadn't cared, actually hoping her mom would end up behind bars. If she was in prison, Sara wouldn't have to worry so much or deal with her. Her mom was one promise she regretted making.

Liam touched her hand, and a jolt went through her. "What were you just thinking about?"

She was wide awake now. "Not going to jail. I share the same intense desire."

The way he looked at her made her wonder if he

wasn't buying what she was selling. "Right. Uh, I'm going to lift weights in about an hour. Would you mind keeping me company?"

"I thought you wanted me to leave you alone?" She smiled and tipped the glass of orange juice up to take a sip. Gosh, he sure was good-looking. His long, dark red hair was just begging for her hands to comb through it, and he had a million-dollar smile. Or billion-dollar, in his case.

She choked and coughed so hard she couldn't breathe. Running to the sink, she brushed herself off with a towel. What an idiot. If only it wasn't said in her mother's voice. Why did it have to be her voice? She dropped the towel and braced her hands on the counter. Composure. She needed it and quick.

"Hey," Liam said and touched her arm.

"Oh." She jumped. "I'm sorry. The juice went down the wrong way."

His eyebrows drew together. "Is everything okay? You looked kind of upset there for a second."

"It was the juice. I'm okay." He had to stop touching her. This was a job. He was a client. This wasn't the time or place for tingles and butterflies, but, boy, did she have them. There was a swarm and a half of butterflies in her stomach at that moment, and her skin was tingling where he touched her.

He nodded and backed his wheelchair up. "Okay."

As she walked back to the table, she asked, "Do you work out every day?"

"At least five days a week. I don't really keep count, but I can feel it if I skip too many days." He stopped his wheelchair at the table and finished off his eggs and waffles.

Her eyebrows shot up. "I honestly didn't believe you could eat all that."

His shoulders bounced as he laughed. "I'm a football player."

"Yes, and now you're a stuffed one. They could sell you in the gift shop." She smiled wide.

Liam shook his head. "Funny. I'm still hungry, by the way."

Her jaw dropped. "What? You ate enough for a family of eight."

"Or one football player."

"I hope you have your heart checked on a regular basis." She could do it. Only she wasn't thinking with a stethoscope. Okay, that was it. Another errant thought like that, and she was going to start pinching herself every time.

The smile he shot her was sexy as all get out. "As a matter of fact, I do."

WHAT ON EARTH was he doing? Flirting with her? *Keep it in check, man!* his head screamed. His heart hummed like it was singing along with an eighties ballad. It was like he couldn't stop himself. Her eyes were killer. Her smile was spectacular. He found himself truly enjoying her company.

In four days, the two weeks of misery had turned into two weeks of "this isn't so bad." She was easy to talk to when she loosened up. He liked the way her nose wrinkled when she laughed.

"Do you mind if I get a shower before you work out?"

"You haven't eaten anything."

She gave him a deadpan look. "I have too. Just because I can't wolf the contents of an entire grocery dairy case doesn't mean I haven't eaten."

His head fell back as he laughed. How long had it been since he laughed like that? It was all the way to the pit of his stomach. He'd found himself laughing a lot more since she'd arrived. Man, he liked her. How many times had he been on a date, wishing for something like this? An intelligent, witty, interesting woman with a great laugh, and beautiful to boot. "I can't eat *that* much."

"But you aren't far behind." She winked.

Whoa. Talk about waking up. His pulse doubled in an instant. "Go get your shower, and I'll clean up here."

She shook her head. "Nope."

"What?"

"I can stay and help clean up. Where I'm from, if you cook, you don't clean up." She smiled.

He crossed his arms over his chest. For the last year, he'd been waited on hand and foot, and it felt good to feel useful to someone. "No, I can do it. I owe you for being such a jerk the first day."

Sara tilted her head and held his gaze almost long enough to make him uncomfortable. "Okay," she said and stood.

What? That was too easy. "You aren't going to argue?"

"No, you want to feel needed." She bent down until she was eye-level. Her fingers threaded through the length of his hair. "You were a football player, free and able to go and do what you wanted. I can't imagine how you must feel."

His mouth felt like a field in a drought. "Um." That's all he had? Um?

A little smile played on her lips. "You know, when you aren't being a grouch, you're kinda cute." She stood, and as she walked out of the kitchen, she shot him a look over her shoulder. "I'll see you in a few minutes."

What had just happened? It was like she could read his mind. She was either really good at her job, or he looked desperate. He didn't doubt she was good at her job. But more than likely, he was pathetic-looking. Did she see him as pathetic? That thought ruffled him.

He looked in the direction of her room, and when he was sure she wasn't coming back out, he stood and started snatching the plates off the table and taking them to the sink. Anger filled him as he walked back and forth from the dining room table.

Pathetic. That's what he was. Pretending to be wheelchair-bound so he didn't have to deal with what was really bothering him. Why couldn't he get over it? The hit had been hard, but no harder than any other he'd taken. He'd even been hurt before. What was it about that hit and this injury that was so paralyzing?

Before he knew it, the table was cleaned off, and the dishes were done. Anger had a way of propelling him to work harder and faster. He braced his hands on the edge of the counter and gripped it until his knuckles were white.

A rattle of a door, and he ran to the wheelchair. She couldn't be done that quickly, or had it been that long? He took a deep breath, and the fresh scent of rain and some fruity mixture swirled around him as she stepped into the kitchen.

"Place looks great."

"What, you didn't think I could do the dishes? I'm in a wheelchair, not helpless," he snapped.

Sara smiled and walked to him. "No, I think I'm terrible at dishes, and it's probably a good thing you didn't let me help."

There was that composure. Maybe she could teach him some of that. "I'm sorry."

"Your bark is a whole lot worse than your bite. Did you know that?" She caught her bottom lip between her teeth, and he sucked in a sharp breath.

Liam rubbed his knuckles down his jaw. "I'm really sorry. I'm just frustrated with myself, and I seem to take it out on other people who have nothing to do with it."

"I know." She tapped him on the nose. "I thought you needed to work out."

Whoa. Yeah, like right now. After, he'd take a long shower, and depending on how things went while he worked out, it could be hot or cold. Really, really cold. "Yeah." His voice was an octave higher than normal.

CHAPTER 8

*R*olling over, Liam grabbed the clattering phone off his nightstand. "Hello?" It was another hazy day. He could almost smell another snow storm coming in.

"Hey, babe."

Katarina Roth. "What do you want?"

"I want to see you, sweetie."

"You dumped me, remember? It was very public. You dumped water over my head and stormed away in the middle of a benefit for Doctors Without Borders."

"I was upset. It wasn't for real." Her chirpy little voice was even more annoying now. It wasn't soft and sweet like Sara's. Oh great. Now he was comparing other women to her?

He covered his eyes with his hand and exhaled. "It's

been over a month since you spoke to me. I think that pretty much screams *for real.*"

"Well, I'm in town, and I'm coming over."

"What?" He sat up straight. "You're in town?"

"Not completely, completely. I'll be there soon, though. I can't wait to see you, babe."

No. He didn't want her to come to his home. "We aren't together anymore, Katarina. Why are you coming here?"

"I want to see you. I've missed your squishy face and spending time with you."

"You told me I was boring, boorish, and beneath you. You said you were sick of my wheelchair and you wanted a real man who could stand up." He wasn't mad at her, he just wanted to be done. Until she called, he wasn't aware they weren't done.

"But, baby, I miss you. I'm already on the plane. I land in an hour."

A headache was building behind his eyes from just talking to her. His head would probably explode if he actually saw her. "I don't think it's a good idea."

"Are you telling me you don't want to see me?"

"Yeah, pretty much."

She sniffed. "I said I'm sorry. Please let me come to the house. We can talk. If we can't make up, I'll leave, and that'll be it."

"You're going to come anyway, aren't you?" She'd done it before. Why not this time?

"Well, I'm desperate. I want to see you."

He raked his hand through his hair. "Fine. We'll talk, but we're done, Katarina. There is no us anymore."

"I'll see you soon," she said and made kissing noises.

That was definitely not happening. In fact, he was thinking he needed his head examined for going out with her in the first place.

He took a deep breath, and the smell of something savory made his mouth water. Whatever was coming from the kitchen, he was eating it. He pulled off the covers, plopped down in the wheelchair, and rolled out of his room.

The smell was like little fingers pulling him by the nose. "I hope you cooked a few pounds of whatever that is."

"It's an egg casserole. It's nothing fancy."

He wheeled himself into the kitchen. "It smells fantastic. Did I have those ingredients?"

"Yes, I hope it's okay that I used them. If you had other plans, I can go into town and replace them." She turned and smiled.

Oh boy. He liked her smile way too much. "Oh, no,

I'm not complaining at all. All I ask is that you give me the recipe."

"I will. I promise."

He didn't want to tell her about Katarina, but it would be worse if she showed up without warning. "My ex-girlfriend is coming later. She's just showing up."

"She wasn't very kind to you, was she? You've had a lot of people not really think about what you want, haven't you?"

"Um."

Sara captured her bottom lip between her teeth. "You say that a lot."

"Um." Because when she did that, he couldn't think. "Well, I, uh, yeah. People don't really ask me what I want. They ask, expecting me to give them the answer they want."

"Let's eat breakfast, and we'll see what we can do about your ex, okay?" She winked.

She could ask him to bake biscuits in the middle of Times Square in his underwear, and he'd probably say yes, especially when she did that. "Okay." He needed to snap out of it. Nurse, she was his nurse. That's it. And he didn't even want a nurse to start with.

They ate together, and he spilled his guts about Katarina. He wasn't even planning on it, it just poured out. One minute he was sitting there, and wham, he had diarrhea of the mouth.

Once breakfast was over, they each hit the showers and met back up in the living room. She never told him what they were going to do about Katarina. It would have helped if he'd asked, but he didn't really care as long as she was there.

His phone buzzed in his pocket, and he checked it. "She's here, pulling into the driveway now."

Sara looked at him. "I have an idea. Do you trust me?"

"Um." He heard the clack of high heels on the front porch and looked at Sara. "Yeah."

"Just go with it, okay?"

"Okay." What was she…

She sat down on his lap and pulled his lips down to hers. Little zaps of electricity pulsated through him. This wasn't a good plan. His head was screaming, *Danger*, while his heart was saying, *Go for it*. He could even hear football fans cheering in the background and see fat guys with "score" written on their stomachs.

Her lips moved against his, and she ran her fingers through his beard, along his cheek, and buried them in his hair.

Whoa. He wrapped his arms around her and held

her. He hadn't felt this good in a long time. He deepened the kiss just as the door opened, and Katarina gasped.

"Baby, what's this?"

He could barely hear her. Honestly, if she left, he wouldn't even care. Sara caressed his cheek with her fingertips and brushed her lips across his as the kiss came to an end. An end he didn't really want.

"Babe?"

He kept his eyes on Sara and kept giving her little kisses. "We broke up." This was so dangerous.

Sara pulled away and smiled. "I guess I should go so you two can talk. I'll see you later, sweetheart." She winked, got up, and disappeared down the hall.

His whole body was trembling, and his head was swimming. It was the best kiss he'd ever had. If that was a fake make out, then he was down for the real thing. Wait. No. Nurse. That's what she was: his nurse. That was it.

SARA SLIPPED into her bedroom and shut the door. She leaned back against it and looked up. *Holy* guacamole, could that man kiss. There would be no more of that. She had to make sure of it. He was a client.

If he needed help in the romance department, he'd have to find someone else. Liam had "heartbreaker" written all over him. He was attractive, flirty, he could be downright sweet and charming, and he knew all of that too.

She pushed off the door and walked to the bed, collapsing face-first into it. What was she thinking, kissing him? So what if his ex-girlfriend showed up? He was a grown man. He should be able to tell her to get to steppin' and wave as she went.

It was a great kiss, though. His lips were soft, and when he was looking at her and kissing her, his gaze was so intense. For a moment, she got lost in it. It wasn't hard to picture herself cradled in his arms, her hands buried in his hair, and kissing him until her lips were bruised.

Her phone rang, and she dreaded looking at it. Why couldn't her mom give her any peace? A knock came from the door, and it felt like she'd been saved. When Sara called her back, she'd have a good reason why she hadn't answered.

Sara went to the door and opened it. Katarina stood there with her arms crossed over her chest. This woman had the longest legs she'd ever seen, and she was gorgeous. Black hair, dark eyes, and creamy skin. "Liam tells me you two are an item."

"Uh, well, if he said it, then it must be true." She smiled.

Katarina's jaw flexed. "Liam is mine. You'd be wise to remember that."

It was quickly becoming clear that rich people were nuts. "Does Liam know he's yours?"

"He had a phone call he had to take. I thought I'd come talk to you, woman to woman." She lifted one perfectly trimmed eyebrow.

"Well, okay. What exactly is it we need to talk about?" What about "over" was she not getting?

"Katarina?" Liam called.

"Let's finish this out there." Her voice was dripping with contempt. How could she be mad that he moved on when she hadn't spoken to him in a month?

Sara nodded and followed her into the living room. The promise to take care of him included making sure ex-girlfriends didn't steamroll him.

"You're an item," Katarina said and waved her hand at Sara, "with this?" She rolled her eyes and exhaled sharply.

Liam narrowed his eyes. "She's attractive, witty, intelligent, and I enjoy her company. I'll gladly take her any day."

The compliment made her cheeks heat. She knew

he was only saying it because he wanted Katarina to go away, but still, it was nice hearing it.

"I said I was sorry. We've always worked it out before. Why not this time?" She huffed.

He drew his eyebrows together and shook his head. "Because I don't want to. This is the fifth or sixth time you've done something like this. I don't want to do it anymore. I want something real, someone real."

There went that eyebrow again. Katarina looked at Sara, and she could almost feel the daggers hitting her. "You know you'll never fit in his world, right? You're one step above a maid. I bet you do his dry cleaning and make dinner."

Oh, this girl was about to get her butt handed to her. "No, I am not. I have hundreds of hours of medical training and eight years of experience. I maintained the highest grades possible and graduated at the top of my class. I can assure you the last thing you want me doing is getting your dry cleaning. And you most definitely don't want me cooking anything for you, especially after you've insulted me." Sara spun on her heels and walked down the hall, darting into her room and shutting the door.

That chick was a walking, talking nightmare. And he dated her? What could he have seen in her, anyway?

Loud voices came from the living room, and then

the front door slammed. It was the kind of slam that meant she wasn't coming back, or at least hopefully wasn't coming back.

There was a light knock on her door, and she opened it. "I kind of lost it on her."

"With good reason. She was being nasty," Liam said and rubbed the back of his neck. "Um, look, about that kiss. It didn't mean anything. You know that, right? I was playing along." He looked at her like he was half-expecting her to swoon because the great Liam had kissed her.

Some nerve. It was a good kiss, but it wasn't that good. Okay, that was a lie, but still. The only reason she kissed him was to make his ex-girlfriend go away. "So, you think a single kiss will have me fawning over you?"

"Well no, I just have to be careful. In the past, women have gotten the wrong impression. I'm famous, wealthy, and…"

Sara felt the heat race to her cheeks and climb up her ears. So what if he played football. And money? That was like waving a red flag in front of a bull.

Bending down, she got eye level with him, and he leaned back, wide-eyed. "I'll have you know I'm not some weak-kneed little fangirl who swoons at your very presence." She poked him in the chest. "And your money means nothing to me. In fact, of your attributes, I find *that* to be the least appealing."

She stepped back, lifted her head up, and looked down her nose at him. Her teeth were grinding so hard the enamel was in danger of flaking off. "Do you need anything at the moment?"

"No."

"Fantastic." She turned and slammed the door. It was all she could do to keep from opening the door and throwing something at him.

The phone began ringing again, and she hung her head. She didn't have it in her to deal with her mom, but if she didn't answer, it would be worse next time.

Picking up the phone, she put it on speaker and laid it on the bed. "Hello, Mom. Are you okay?" At least this way she could use both hands to pull her hair out.

CHAPTER 9

"I need you to come get me."

Music played in the background, and she could almost smell the cigarette smoke coming through the phone. "Where are you?"

"You aren't at home, and I'm bored, so I decided I need to get out and have a little fun. Are you going to come get me?"

"I can't. I'm working."

"Then what am I supposed to do?"

Jump off a cliff? "I'll call you a cab as soon as I get off the phone. I can't leave. I promised his sister I'd take care of him. I can't break my promise to her." She sighed.

"Him?" her mom said, and it seemed she'd perked up.

Great. "You know I can't talk about it. Aside from the fact that I signed a confidentiality agreement, I don't talk about my clients."

"You can tell me. I'm your mother."

"I can't tell anyone. I won't tell anyone. He deserves his privacy." Even if she hadn't signed the agreement, she wouldn't tell her mom. Liam was beyond wealthy. If her mom found out she was working for Liam Thomas, it'd be like putting a bulls-eye on him.

"I bet he's some rich thing. You should do like me and land yourself a big fish. Let him take care of you. You could have had that with Chris, but no. You had to be stupid."

Oh, she was definitely drunk. Sara gritted her teeth. How many times had she asked her to stop talking to her like that? "Please don't call me names."

"Why? You are. You left him. He had money. What were you thinking?"

"Money isn't everything. Chris was cruel. He hurt me; don't you remember? I couldn't stay with him. I don't care how much money he won." Chris wasn't great before the money, and the wealth brought out his worst traits, like his temper.

"See, I knew you were an idiot. He won twenty million dollars. All you had to do was play nice, and you could have been set...and so could I."

Living large. Yeah, because money fixed everything. "I don't want to be set. I want to find someone who will love me. Someone I can take care of and who'll take care of me. Someone who's sweet and funny." Liam's face floated to her mind, and she rubbed her temple. That was not going to happen. She pinched her arm so hard she thought she'd have a bruise. That would teach her.

"That's where you're an idiot—"

"Mom, please don't call me that."

"Well, you are. And you didn't leave me enough money. If you were worth anything, you'd make more money."

"Mom, you're being mean. Please stop."

"I'm so sick of you. You and your stupid high-and-mighty self. Acting like you're better than everyone. You're just worthless. I hate you. I wish I'd never had you."

Sara sank to the floor and laid her head against the side of the mattress. What she wouldn't give to go back and not make that promise. But she couldn't break it. Other than the car, it was all she had left of her dad. He was the one who instilled in her the meaning of a promise. *Don't ever promise something and not deliver. If you don't think you can do, don't. But if you do, be prepared to work to keep it.* Part of her still held out hope that one day her mom would change and she'd love her.

"You know I didn't want you, right? When your dad died, they kept calling, begging me to take you. I did, and look at the thanks I get."

She needed her mom off the phone. "There's a little more money in one of the magazines in the drawer by the stove. If you're careful, it should be enough to get you through until I come home."

There was a little shuffling, and when her mom spoke, her voice was a little higher. "There is?"

"Yes, I was saving it for a rainy day. Please make it last." She pressed the flat of her hand against her forehead. "I have to go. I've already been on the phone too long."

"You just don't want to talk to me; that's all. You hate me."

"No, I don't hate you. I can't be on the phone when I'm working."

"Fine. I didn't want to talk to you anyway." The phone went dead.

Sara covered her face with her hands, and her body trembled as she sobbed. Why was this time hitting her so hard? It wasn't anything she hadn't heard before. For some reason, it felt like her mom had torn her to shreds. Emotionally, she was shot.

A knock on the door sobered her, and she looked over her shoulder. The door hadn't fully shut when she slammed it, and she could see Liam through a small crack. "Yes, Mr. Thomas? Can I help you?" Normally, she'd go to the door, but she wasn't going to let him see her like that again.

"I wanted to apologize. I'm kind of a dumb jerk sometimes, and I have a habit of sticking my foot in my mouth."

That was one way to put it. "It's okay. I know you're frustrated. You probably do have a lot of people who want to take advantage of you. I apologize for my outburst."

"No, I had that coming. You were a little scary, though."

She chuckled. He had the charm thing down. Bad news was what he was: lots of bad news and heartache. "I'm short but mighty."

"I really am sorry. You should probably get it on recording so we can speed up the process." He laughed.

Her talking quota had been met for the day. All she wanted was to be left alone. "Is there anything I can do for you, Mr. Thomas?"

"No, I mostly wanted to apologize." He paused. "And you can call me Liam."

"I think it's probably best if we keep with the formalities, Mr. Thomas." There. Even in a haze of tears and in an emotional black pit, she'd kept her wits and fixed whatever he might have thought was going on.

"Okay."

The tires squeaked on the floor as he spun the chair and wheeled away.

She closed her eyes and sagged against the bed. It was like she couldn't catch a break. Why couldn't things be easy just once? If she ever got an answer, she hoped it would make sense.

As she sat there, the toll of the day dragged her down, and she fell asleep.

LIAM ROLLED onto his back and stared up at the ceiling. He'd been such an idiot. Why couldn't his brain work when she was around? *You know that kiss didn't mean anything, right?* He'd seen the fire light in her eyes faster than dryer lint in the fireplace.

She'd scared him with the way she'd bent down and curled her lips. He didn't want to be on the business end of Sara Lynch.

Then he'd gone to her room to apologize, and she

was talking to her mom. How much abuse could one person take? And she just sat there, calm, composed, and never raising her voice. She'd earned even more of his respect with that phone call.

What kind of mom told their kid they didn't want them? How many times had Sara heard that? She'd fallen to the floor by then and had laid her head against the bed. He'd never wanted to hold someone so badly in his life.

He liked her. More than liked her. She didn't deserve to be treated like that. He needed to stop treating her like that. How had he been any different? With thoughts like those, he was never getting to sleep.

Throwing the covers off, he slipped into his wheelchair. Maybe he'd sit by the fireplace and try to figure out what he needed to do. He wheeled himself out of his room and stopped as he heard little cries.

Roughly a foot from the fireplace, Sara sat with her knees drawn to her chest and her arms wrapped around her legs. Her head was down, and her body was shaking. He could tell she was desperately trying to hold sobs in.

"Sara." He said her name as he approached.

She quickly turned away. "Yes, Mr. Thomas, can I help you?"

"Are you okay?" It was obvious she wasn't, but he didn't know a better way to start the conversation.

"I'm fine. Is there something you need?" There was no missing the tremble in her voice.

"Other than to find out why you're crying? No." He wheeled closer.

Sara wiped her eyes with the hem of her shirt and turned. "I'm fine."

"Your puffy red eyes say otherwise." He shot her a smile.

She straightened. Robot Business Sara was back on the job. "I don't think it's a good idea to mix personal stuff with the professional. Kissing you earlier was a clear demonstration it shouldn't happen again."

Liam pulled himself out of the chair, onto the edge of the fireplace, and then worked himself around until he was sitting next to her. "I was a jerk, and you were doing me a favor. You did nothing wrong. I wasn't exactly fighting you off, if you'll recall." And if he was honest, he was more than enjoying it. The kiss had meant something. Then he'd shot his mouth off and messed it up.

"I've never been this unprofessional in my entire career. I can't seem to do anything right, lately." She crossed her arms over her knees and laid her forehead against them. "I'm so tired."

He nodded. "I think I can understand how you're feeling. I haven't exactly been the model for good decisions either." Understatement of the year.

With a shrug, Sara lifted her head. "You're frustrated. Something traumatic happened to you, and you're still trying to process it. I doubt your hip even hurts anymore. You're trying to figure out what you want to do before you let anyone know, because the moment you do, they'll be circling like vultures." She clamped both hands over her mouth and closed her eyes tightly.

His jaw dropped. How did she do that? He was actually beginning to think she could read minds.

She held her head with her hands. "I'm so sorry. I don't know what's wrong with me."

"Nothing." Because she was right.

"It's not my place to say things like that." She rubbed her forehead with her hand.

He sat quietly for a few moments. "Even when you're right?"

She looked at him. "What?"

"My hip hasn't been hurting for quite some time. I've been trying to figure out why I'm so freaked out about a tackle and injury. It's happened before, so it's nothing new. Why is this one so different?"

"You mean you don't have to be in a wheelchair?

All this time? Why didn't you come clean with your sister? Then you wouldn't be dealing with me."

At the moment, he was beginning to think she was the one good thing that came out of it. "I'm not minding it so much. It's been nice to talk to someone who doesn't want anything from me."

She touched his hip. "It doesn't hurt at all?"

The warmth of her hand spread through the pajama bottoms he was wearing and covered him so fast his brain stuttered. He needed to not screw this up. He shook his head. "No."

"I'm kind of shocked, even though I suspected it." She giggled.

Was she laughing at him? "What?"

She laughed a little harder.

"Okay, now you've got me worried."

"You're a little rat fink." She shook her head. "Well, not little. Massive. You're as big as a house."

He rolled his tongue against the inside of his cheek and stretched his legs in front of him. "I guess I am, on both counts."

"Why didn't you tell your sister?"

He gave a little shrug. "She raised me. Our parents died when I was twelve. Kimberly was eighteen and kind of became like a mom to me. She's proud of my football career. I guess it's kind of like her certificate of good parenting. If I told her, she'd be on me to get back out there, and I'm not ready."

Sara touched his arm. "I'm sorry about your parents, and she's a great sister. You're lucky, but if you aren't ready, you have no business out there. I watched that play over and over. It wasn't just a tackle. It was two large trains colliding head-on. That massive guy really hurt you, and not only your hip. I saw your body take that hit. And if I'm honest, I teared up. I can't imagine what you've been going through."

The spot where her hand touched him tingled. He was dangerously close to taking her in his arms and kissing her again. Talk about a disaster, especially when he'd basically accused her of using him. "I think it's messing with my head."

She twisted to face him, and his breath caught as she combed her fingers through his hair. "Well, of course it did. It was traumatic. You were playing football one minute and being carried off the field the next. You left the stadium unconscious. Anyone would be feeling a little anxious. You're doing great. When you're ready to go back, you'll know it."

How did she do that? Make him feel so relaxed and comfortable while talking to her. It was like she could see through him. Her mesmerizing green eyes locked with his, and his pulse jumped.

Caressing his cheek with her fingers, she said, "I bet you've been in such turmoil, trying to figure out who you are and being stuck in a wheelchair so you can have the time you need to do it."

Sara unnerved the daylights out him. "Pretty much."

She faced the fire again and yawned.

"Tired?"

"Completely shot." She yawned again and leaned her head against his arm.

It shocked him, but he liked it. He really liked her. Why couldn't he like her? He'd had women as friends before. Because, deep down, he knew the potential for something more was there, and it scared him.

Her head fell forward, and she jerked it back up. "I'm sorry."

Before he could stop himself, he put his arm around her shoulder. "It's okay." He found himself thinking he could get used to it, to her. He already felt more comfortable with her than he'd felt with anyone he ever dated. Liam combed his fingers through her hair.

She leaned into him and groaned. "I'm so sorry. I can't keep my eyes open." She chuckled as her eyes closed. "You know, this has been one of the best jobs I've taken."

He froze and then pulled his fingers from her hair and pressed his hand to his forehead. That's right. She'd made a promise to care about him. The way she was treating him wasn't personal; she was his nurse. That's all she was, and that's all she'd be. He had enough on his plate without adding a relationship to the mix, anyway. He'd make sure nothing came of it, even if he had to use a nuclear option to avoid it.

At least now he could walk for the rest of the time his sister was gone. No more hiding for a while. The thought was like fireworks in his soul.

CHAPTER 10

*S*ara pushed herself up in the bed and rubbed her eyes. Through the window, she could see the sun high in the sky. All she remembered from the night before was talking to Liam and then falling asleep. The bus that hit her must have been traveling at light speed.

Never had she slept this late before. Not when she was working. Pushing off the covers, she scrambled out of bed and rushed to the shower. Ever since she started this job, she'd felt out of sorts.

Liam wanted her to relax, but she was too relaxed. As she came out of the shower, she heard loud music. What was going on? She quickly dressed and pulled her hair up. It would just have to stay wet.

She opened the door of her room and walked into the living room.

Liam was sprawled on the couch with the stereo playing full blast. He tipped his head to her and turned down the music. "Oh, hey. About time you woke up. Aren't you supposed to be on the clock?"

Confusion mixed with a little hurt sliced through her. "I apologize. It won't happen again."

"See that it doesn't." His tone was back to being clipped with an edge of anger, like it was the first day she arrived.

The previous night had been great. He'd been so sweet and even confided in her that his hip was healed. When he'd put his arm around her, she thought for sure they'd made progress toward being friends. What could have changed while she was asleep? Part of her wanted to ask, but the hurt she felt was giving way to anger. If this is how he wanted things, then that's what he'd get. "Is there anything I can do for you?"

Liam cleared his throat. "I could use a meal. Think you can manage that?"

She could hear her heart pounding in her ears as the heat raced to the tips of her ears. "Yes, what would you like?"

He shrugged. "I'm sure you can figure something out."

Sara nodded, keeping her gaze trained on the floor. Why was he being so awful? "Is that all?"

"For now," Liam said.

Sara walked to the kitchen and stopped at the counter, holding her stomach. It felt like she'd been gut-punched. How had she been so wrong about his character? After they'd come so far, she would have never believed he'd behave so spiteful.

She handled it when she first got there because she understood he was frustrated, and he had a reason to be. There was no reason to be so hateful now that he didn't have to pretend. And it wasn't *what* he said; it was the cruel tone in his voice that threw her off. For the life of her, she didn't understand why.

"I don't think you're supposed to be standing around," Liam called from the couch.

Without looking at him, she replied, "I'm just trying to come up with something for dinner."

"Right. Just hurry up." Liam turned the music up again.

How could she have misjudged him so badly? What kind of game had he been playing with her? There was no difference between him and Chris. Two men with money, treating her like dirt.

For the next hour, Sara prepared dinner while listening to Liam blare his music, furious at herself for making a promise that kept her from being able to walk out the front door and be done with him.

"Smells like it's done," Liam said as he walked into the kitchen.

"It is," she said and began setting the table.

"Uh, I actually do have some dry cleaning that needs to be taken in tomorrow. I have a gala coming up." He swiped his finger in a dish as she set it on the table.

Sara stopped, clasped her hands in front of her, and looked at him. "That's fine. Leave it on the couch, and I'll take it in the morning."

"Great. Maybe when you get back, you can make the bed too."

Sara blinked hard and looked away. "Will that be all, Mr. Thomas?"

He chuckled. "I'll come get you when I'm done, and you can clean up."

"Okay." She walked out of the kitchen and didn't stop until she was safely behind her bedroom door. She slid down, put her head in her hands, and sobbed.

What had she been thinking, even entertaining being attracted to him? He'd been rude, obnoxious, and cold since she got there. She'd let a few cute apologies cloud her judgment and set her up to be hurt.

That wasn't going to happen again. When she woke up tomorrow, he'd learn how robotic she could be. She'd take Goosey into town, drop off his dry cleaning, and return. One week left, and then she'd be done with this ginormous jerk.

She wondered if Kimberly knew he could be like this. Describing him as wonderful made it clear his sister didn't know her brother as well as she thought. Clearly, she didn't, or she would have known he wasn't hurting anymore. No, he was just doing the hurting.

Not that she'd expected anything more to develop between them, but she'd thought they could be friends. What, exactly, was last night? A joke?

Sara wiped her eyes and stood. He was a client who she needed to detach from. She'd allowed herself to get too close and forget what he was. That was not a mistake she'd be making again anytime soon.

LIAM WOKE up on the couch the next morning just as Sara picked up his tuxedo and draped it over her arm. She didn't look right, but then again, he'd been malicious. It was the only way he could think of to put distance between them. If she hated him, then he was safe. He just didn't calculate how hurt she'd look.

Her gaze found his, and she said, "Is there anything else you'd like me to do while I'm in town?"

"Yeah, you can pick me up something for lunch. Nothing hot. It'd be cold by the time you got back."

"Sure. Anything else?" If Sara was a weather system, she'd be an arctic blast.

Liam dug into his pants and pulled out his keys, tossing them to her. "You can take the AMG."

She walked to the door, and on her way, she dropped them back on him. "No, thank you." And out the door she went.

He flopped back and raked a hand through his hair. She was furious. He'd wanted to make her angry, to push her away. Besides, she was only an employee.

Then again, he hadn't just treated her like an employee. He'd treated her worse than he'd ever treated anyone in his life. He was the guy who rushed in and stopped the guy from hitting someone. He was the one who left a bigger tip than necessary. He was the good guy, but he sure didn't feel good now.

Why had he done it? What had possessed him to behave so unlike himself? The night before, it'd been great to tell her he could walk. He could still picture the way she'd looked at him. How she'd run her fingers through his hair. Then she'd said he was a job, right after it had felt like they'd shared something.

Liam sat up, set his feet on the floor, and put his head in heads. Why did he care that she called him a job? No, not care. Why did it hurt? She was his nurse, and he hadn't even wanted that to begin with.

Why? Because if he was honest with himself, he liked her. It'd felt good to talk with her the night before. She was the most exceptional women he'd ever met—other than his sister.

He stood and paced in front of the couch, more frustrated and confused than he'd been in his life. What was his problem?

Even after hearing the way her mom had treated her, knowing the abuse Sara had suffered, he'd been no better. No, he'd been worse. Her mother was a cruel drunk, and he didn't have that excuse. He'd been stone-cold sober, and the realization cut him to the core.

Sara was witty, sweet, kind, and caring. Her smart-mouth was one of the best things about her. He'd enjoyed her company and the way she wouldn't put up with his nonsense. She was a genuinely good person, and he'd used everything he knew about her against her. The only thing he hadn't done was use what he knew about her mother to hurt her.

Sitting down hard, the reason hit him like a fist to the chest. The night before had given him a glimpse of something good, and he'd run like he was being chased by a bear. A relationship with Sara wouldn't be a fling or casual. Something with her would be life-altering. It'd be deep and powerful, and the idea of having a relationship like that terrified him.

He let his head drop back on the couch and exhaled. He didn't know if he was ready for anything like that. All he knew was that he was an idiot and he'd made a huge mistake.

How on earth was he going to fix this? Could he fix it? Sara was gracious, but even he knew he'd most likely gone too far this time. This *was* what the nuclear option did, wasn't it? He stood and shook his head as he walked to his room. Maybe a long shower would help him figure out what he needed to do.

CHAPTER 11

*S*ara parked Goosey away from the house. Part of her wondered if she could survive sleeping in her. She didn't want to be around Liam, not with him acting like that again. Not with him being hateful. He'd really hurt her this time, and she couldn't figure out why.

The promise she'd made to Kimberly flashed like neon in her mind. In the future, she was going to be more careful about the promises she made. This was the second one coming back to bite her in the rear— her mom being the first.

Once Liam had called, canceling the lunch order, she'd taken her time tooling around town until it was closer to dinner. It had taken her longer to get down the mountain because Goosey's brakes were soft.

When the job was over, she'd have to take her in and have them checked. They were still doing okay, but her heart had pounded a couple of times when she didn't stop like she was supposed to. She'd thought about doing it while she was in town, but she was tired.

Touching her hand to her forehead, she leaned her head back against the seat. The aching feeling from earlier hadn't gone away. It'd gotten worse as the day went on. She'd had to stop on the way to the house and throw up. More than likely, Liam had shared his little bug with her.

Another thing from him she didn't appreciate. With a shake of her head, she got out of the car and dragged herself to the house. She didn't feel good at all. What she needed was a bed and a long, dark night. Hopefully, that started with slipping through the house without coming into contact with Liam.

Yes, she would take care of him, but she didn't have it in her to deal with him at the moment. She stopped in front of the door and leaned her forehead against it, silently praying for a break. What a joke. A break? It would never happen.

Sara took a deep breath and mentally prepared herself for whatever was on the other side, and then she opened the door. Yep, there were no breaks for her. Liam sat in the armchair, facing the door, and he looked up as she stepped inside.

What would be the most professional thing to do? That's how she dealt with situations when she was struggling. "Is there something you need, Mr. Thomas?"

"No, I just..."

"If there's nothing you need, I'll be in my room." She crossed the living room and walked down the hall. Footfalls behind her made her pause at her door.

Liam stopped short. "Can we talk?"

Squaring her shoulders, she turned and looked at him. "Mr. Thomas, is there something you need?"

"I need to talk to you."

What should she do? She didn't want to hear anything he said, but he was still a client, one she'd been stupid enough to let get too close. "What do you need to talk about?"

"I did something stupid. I shouldn't have treated you like that."

It took strength not to laugh. Something stupid? No, more like something showing such a low level of character that she would've never associated it with him. "Is that all?"

"Please, talk to me. Don't go back to Robot Sara. I

made a huge mistake." He seemed to be pleading with his eyes. "I can't tell you how sorry I am."

"Is that all?"

He raked his hand through his hair. "Sara, don't do that."

"Mr. Thomas, I am here to take care of you. I promised your sister I would. If there is nothing else, I will be retiring to my room. Unless you'd like me to prepare your dinner, in which case I'll need to know what you'd like." Whatever friendship he may have thought they'd developed was gone. She would be keeping him at a distance until her time was up.

His shoulders sagged, and he looked nearly distraught. It was only an act, though. She wasn't falling for that again. "No, I don't want you cooking dinner. I want to—"

"Is that all?"

Taking her by the arms, he said, "You're like a broken record. Stop it. I was mean and hateful this morning. I'm sorry. Tell me what I can do to fix it."

"Mr. Thomas, you need to take your hands off of me. If there's nothing else you need, I will see you tomorrow." Her tone was firm.

He released her and stepped back. "I can't fix this, can I?" His voice broke. The sorrow almost made her give in.

No, she wasn't being stupid again. Not where he was concerned. She put her hand on the knob and closed her eyes. All she had to do was hold it together long enough to get into her room. Clenching her jaw, she looked at him and said, "No, you can't." Her lip almost trembled. She slipped inside and shut the door, sagging back against it.

Safety, finally. It was either get inside the room or break down and talk to him. Those puppy dog eyes and the way his voice broke…Man, he wasn't just a good football player, he was a good actor.

For now, she needed to lie down. The sick feeling wasn't going away, and the only good thing for that was sleep. She walked to the bed and let her coat slip from her shoulders and hit the floor. Crawling on top, she collapsed into the softness of the comforter. She was too hot to pull the covers on, so she kicked her shoes off and curled into a ball.

She wasn't sure what she'd done to deserve the things that had happened to her, but she was beginning to think maybe she'd done something horrible and didn't know it. Whatever it was, she was sorry, and if someone would tell her the offense she'd made, she'd do her best to never do it again.

Her eyes slid closed, and with one last deep breath, she drifted to sleep.

Scrubbing his face with his hands, Liam sat on the edge of his bed. The look on Sara's face when she walked into the living room after being gone all day killed him. She may have been trying to hide the hurt and disappointment, but he could see it in her eyes.

Sara was as closed down as Fort Knox. There was no cracking the wall she'd put up. He wasn't even going to have another chance to be her friend. The way she'd looked at him when she'd said he couldn't fix it broke his heart. He wasn't supposed to be developing feelings for her. But he was, and it scared him.

She was the best thing to happen to him in a long time, and he hadn't pushed her away; he'd shoved. He had no good explanation either. Well, other than fear. He'd dated a woman who he'd thought he wanted forever with, only to find out it had been one-sided. It had shut him down. Sure, he'd dated, but it was surface-type dating. Like being a meat-and-potatoes kind of guy and settling for the salad bar. What if Sara didn't think that way about him? Could he handle finding out his feelings were one-sided again? Especially when these feelings had the potential to be deeper than he'd felt for anyone?

A clink came from the kitchen, and he looked up.

Sara was awake. He looked at the clock. Three a.m.? What was she doing up? He stood and walked out of his room to the kitchen.

Her hair was wet, and she was wearing a thin pair of pajama pants and a short-sleeved t-shirt. She had her back to him, and her hands were braced on the counter. "I apologize for waking you up." She paused, putting her fingers to her temple. "I was getting a glass for water and almost...dropped it."

"It's okay. You didn't wake me up." He crossed the kitchen and stopped next to her. "Are you okay?"

She looked up at him. Her cheeks were rosy, and her eyes were dull. He'd noticed the tint in her cheeks earlier in the evening, but he'd chalked it up to anger. "I'm fine. Is there anything I can do for you?"

Robotic Sara. He hated it. He wanted witty, laughing Sara back. Of the horrible things he'd done in his life, his stupid stunt was at the top of the list.

"You don't look fine." He reached out to touch her, and she flinched back.

The hard look she gave him cut him to the core. "I'm a nurse, and I can take care of myself. Is there anything I can do for you, Mr. Thomas?"

He shook his head. "No."

She took one hand off the counter, paused, and then dropped her other hand to her side. "Then I'll be going. If you need me, I'll be in my room." Something was way off with the way she was moving.

"Sara, I—"

Her hand went up. "I have your apology on recording."

His stomach hit the floor so hard it bounced. What prayer could he say that could maybe help him find a chink in that armor of hers?

She turned and crossed the kitchen, stopping just before the living room. "If you need anything, don't hesitate to ask."

"Wait. You didn't get your water." He grabbed the glass, filled it, and took it to her.

She kept her head down. "I'll come back for it."

"Sara."

When she lifted her gaze, stormy green eyes met his. "I can take care of myself. I've been doing it since I was eight." She closed her eyes and swayed.

He didn't care how angry she was with him, she was sick. Setting the glass on the kitchen table, he said, "I know you're angry with me, but—"

"You're assuming too much."

Fine. She was ticked. He put his arm around her back, pulled her to him, and pressed his hand to her forehead. "You're burning up. You can barely stand. You need help."

She pushed against him. "I don't. I just need to lie down. I'm fine." Her teeth chattered, and she shivered.

"You did say you were stubborn." Scooping her up, he took her to her room and laid her on the bed. "I'll be back."

"Don't."

He rolled his eyes and walked out of the room. A few minutes later, he returned with a bowl of cold water, a cloth, and the glass of water. She may not want his help, but she was getting it anyway.

Why had he been so stupid? He'd enjoyed spending time with her. When was the last time that happened with a woman? Long enough that he couldn't remember.

Liam sat beside her on the bed and touched her cheek with the back of his hand. Then he noticed the thermometer sitting on her nightstand. "How high is your temperature?"

She pushed on him. "Leave me alone."

"Answer me."

She pinched her lips together and looked away. Okay, she had him beat in the stubborn game.

He slid his arm around her back and pulled her up. Holding her face with his hand so she had to look at him, he said, "You have every right to be angry with me, but you can't take care of yourself this time. You need help. What was your temperature?"

"A hundred and three."

Way too high. "Have you taken anything?"

Her eyes were half-closed, and he could feel the heat coming from her skin. "No. I was getting the water to do that."

"And you were going to leave without it?" He laid her back down, dipped the cloth in the water, and put it on her forehead.

She exhaled and closed her eyes, putting her hand on the cloth. "I don't want to be around you. You hurt me. I thought you were different. I misjudged you."

Talk about a kick to the gut. "No, you didn't. I'm just a moron."

"That goes without saying."

He smiled. Man, she had a quick wit. "You have a smart-mouth."

She opened her eyes and looked at him. "Among other things." The smile she gave him was thin.

"What do you need to get this fever down?"

"Acetaminophen and Ibuprofen. The combination should bring it down."

"No cold-water sponge bath?" He couldn't resist.

Another thin smile. "In your dreams."

He grinned and shook his head. "I'll be back." He

quickly stood and hurried across the house. What would have happened if he hadn't heard her in the kitchen? If her temperature went any higher, she could have been in serious trouble. It made his stupid stunt that much worse.

With medicine in hand, he headed back to her room and poured out two of each. He lifted her again, dropped them in her mouth, and put the glass to her lips. She didn't stop drinking until the glass was empty. "So much for waiting on that water," he said.

"I would have been fine."

"What's your definition of fine?"

She held his gaze. "Alone."

"Smart-aleck."

"Jerk."

His mouth dropped open. She'd yet to say anything remotely like that. "Just how sick are you?"

"Enough that you're attractive again."

Liam chuckled and laid her down. "Do you want some more water?"

"No."

He brushed his fingertips across her cheek. "Is there anything else I can get you or do for you?"

Tears pooled in her eyes, and she looked away. "I don't want to like you anymore."

Boy, did he deserve that. "I know, but what can I do for you?"

She looked up at him. "You disappointed me."

"I'm disappointed in me too."

Pushing up on her elbow, she knitted her eyebrows together. "Why were you so mean to me this morning? What did I do?"

He hung his head. "Nothing. I...don't know why."

"You don't even have a reason?" Her voice broke as she asked, and he jerked his head up. Her eyes were glassy, and the look on her face made him feel lower than dirt.

What could he say? *I think I'm developing feelings for you, and it's freaking me out?* He couldn't say that. He was smart enough to know that. "I'm a stupid guy."

"Yeah," she said and dropped back on the bed.

Instead of responding, he took the cloth from her forehead and rewet it. He didn't have an adequate response. He regretted it. He was sorry and wished he'd never done it, but he'd already said that. Repeating it would be useless. His only hope was that she was more forgiving than he was stupid.

CHAPTER 12

*A*s the sun poured in through the window, a tickle on the end of Liam's nose woke him up as he rested next to Sara widthwise on the bed. She was on her back with her face pointed at him and her eyes closed. The last eight hours had been tough, and the rosiness in her cheeks hadn't lessened even a little. Her fever was holding on with two hands.

She half-opened her eyes, and a sliver of dull green met his. "I'm hot."

"Yeah, you are." He smiled.

She licked her lips. "I don't feel good."

No smart response? He touched her forehead and sat up to grab the thermometer off the nightstand. He put it in her mouth and when it beeped, he knew why. "It's almost a hundred and five."

"Lukewarm water to bring it down." Her eyes slid closed. "I don't have the energy to move."

He picked her up, briskly walked to the shower, and turned the water on. As soon as it wasn't freezing, he stepped in with her, letting her feet dangle as he held her around the waist. The second the water hit her, she sucked in a sharp breath, and her body began trembling.

"I've n-n-never been this sick b-b-before. I'm s-s-sorry."

Shaking his head, he said, "You're sorry for being sick? I gave it to you."

Thirty heartbeats. "True. You should a-a-apologize."

At least her fever was coming down. He hefted her up so she could lean her head against his shoulder, and she circled her arms around his neck.

Her lips moved against his skin. "Promise me you won't ever do that again." She said it so softly he almost didn't hear her.

If he wasn't holding her, he'd do a cartwheel. "I promise. Never, ever again." He hoped she'd remember the conversation.

He kept Sara under the water until he was positive she was out of danger. "Do you think you can change your clothes?" he asked as he laid her on the bed. Her cheeks weren't near as red as earlier.

She smiled, and he knew she was about to say something smart. "You keep holding me, and now you're trying to take my clothes off. Is there something you need to tell me?"

Liam chuckled and felt the heat rush to his cheeks. "I'm going to go change my clothes. I'll be back."

He left her room and walked straight to his, shaking his head and smiling. Whoever was smiling down on him had his eternal gratitude. She was feeling better, and she wasn't hating him. His hope was that it'd last. Her friendship was worth everything to him.

Changing as quickly as he could into some sweats and a t-shirt, he strode back to her room, knocking on the frame as he stopped just outside. "Are you dressed?"

"Yes." Her voice was soft.

He stepped inside and found her in dry clothes, holding on to the dresser as she stood next to it.

"No sponge, but I did get that cold-water bath. Joke's on me, huh?" She chuckled.

Oh, he liked her. He more than liked her, but he wasn't ready for something like that with her. She was someone you held on to and never let go. She was a forever woman. He walked to her and picked her up.

"You're holding me again."

He rolled his tongue along the inside of his cheek, and he grinned. "Could you have made it to the bed?"

She wrapped her arms around his neck. "Not without breaking my face."

"Then I guess it's a good thing I'm holding you again," he said as he laid her on the bed and then stretched out next to her. There was no way he was leaving her, not while she had a fever.

With her eyes closed, Sara rolled onto her side and curled her hands under chin. Silence filled the room, and he thought she'd fallen asleep. "I can't sleep," she said, and her eyes opened. "Talk to me."

"Am I so boring I'll knock you out? Is that what you're trying to say?" As she rolled onto her back, he scooted closer and propped his head in his hand.

A little smile. "Yes."

He chuckled. "I've never had anyone make me laugh like you do."

"I like seeing you smile. You have a freckle that peeks out from your mustache right above your lip, and it's cute."

It was a good thing he was lying down, or he'd have fallen down. Boy, she *was* sick. He couldn't imagine her ever saying something like that if she wasn't. "It is, huh?"

She nodded and brushed her thumb over his lip. "Right there."

He hated her being sick, but if she hadn't been, he wasn't sure he could've fought the temptation to kiss her. "Well, you're cute all over."

Her gaze lowered for a moment, and when she looked back up, her bottom lip was caught between her teeth.

"And that right there is just...wrong." And it did things to him he couldn't explain.

She looked at him like he'd spoken a foreign language. "What?"

"Nothing. Are you going to be mad at me when you're thinking straight?" He wasn't sure he wanted to know the answer, especially when he wanted the answer to be no.

"I want to be." Her eyes closed, and her words were slurred.

"I deserve it, but I hope you won't." There was no answer. She'd drifted to sleep. "Please don't be Robot Sara when you wake up." He bent down and kissed her forehead. "Please."

~

STRETCHING AWAKE THE NEXT DAY, Sara opened her eyes and found Liam lying next to her, asleep. She almost startled until she remembered he'd taken care of her while she was sick. Why couldn't she stay mad at him? He'd hurt her. Not only because he treated her like a maid, but because of the way he'd done it. The cruel way he'd spoken to her.

She was so out of her element. Nothing like this had ever happened to her before. She'd never been that sick in her life. If he hadn't been there, or if he'd left her, she wasn't sure what would have happened. She'd never developed feelings for a client before either. It was against the rules she'd created for herself when she started her career. The agency frowned upon it as well.

What was she going to do? Could she be friends with him and cut it off there? She certainly didn't want to be mad at him anymore. It wasn't a lie when she said she liked him. It was fun to make him laugh. She liked his smile and the way his eyes would sparkle.

Friends. That's all they could be. If she could maintain her cool in hard situations, she could do that. Maybe. As she lay there, she studied his face, and all she wanted to do was kiss him. She shook her head, trying to chase the crazy thought away.

Liam took a deep breath and blinked awake. "Are

you feeling better?"

"Yes."

He held her gaze and took a small breath. "Please don't be Robot Sara." There was a slight tremble in his voice.

She lifted on her elbow and kissed his cheek. "Thank you for taking care of me."

"You aren't mad at me anymore?" He'd certainly mastered the puppy dog look...an Irish Setter puppy dog look.

"No. I wasn't angry as much as I was hurt, but I've seen people do horrible things to others, not realizing the ramifications of their actions. I'm going to apply that to you." She brushed the back of her hand along his cheek.

He pulled her to him and hugged her tightly. It was like he'd been holding his breath, waiting for her answer. His arms stayed around her as he leaned back. "Thank you."

"What happened to make you behave like that?"

His eyebrows drew together, and his lips pursed. It was like he was having a war with himself. "I wish I had an answer for you, but I don't. All I can say is I'm sorry."

She looked down. Why didn't he have an answer for her? Maybe opening up the night before had scared him. PTSD and the emotional turmoil that came with it wasn't straightforward. Could it have been that telling her he was well had opened a can of worms that he thought he was ready for and wasn't? He'd been so isolated and smothered over the last year, confiding in her could have been too much for him, and he maybe didn't even realize that's what it was.

When she looked back up, he was staring straight at her, and the energy between them had shifted. Electricity popped and crackled. Her pulse was climbing so fast she felt light-headed.

Her stomach growled, and heat lit up her cheeks. She was embarrassed but thankful. Kissing him again would've been the wrong thing to do. "I guess I'm hungry."

Liam smiled and laughed. "Would you want to go get a burger?"

Her mouth watered at the mention of it. "Yeah. That sounds really good."

"Meet you in the living room in twenty." He kissed her forehead and stood.

The heat in her cheeks turned up a degree. "Okay."

One last look and he was out the door, shutting it behind him. She touched her forehead where he'd kissed her. Her fever hadn't been as hot. Friends. They could be friends. That's it.

CHAPTER 13

The most comfortable thing Sara could find was a pair of old sweats with a hole in the knee and a large, baggy t-shirt. If she had something a little less frumpy with similar comfort, she'd wear it. She just wasn't up to blouse-and-slacks attire yet.

One last grumble at the mirror, and she walked into the living room where Liam was waiting for her. Of course, he'd look great. Jeans, long-sleeved button-up, and looking like he'd just posed for a magazine.

"You want me to drive?" he asked.

"I look that bad?" She chuckled. "I guess I do. I feel better just…"

He shot her a half-smile. "Worn out?"

"A little, but I can drive."

"I can drive," Liam said.

"Do you want people to think you're not in your wheelchair anymore?"

His eyebrows kneaded together. "No."

"Okay, then I'll drive." She held her finger up. "Hold on."

There was no way she was going back to that burger place where her mom was with him looking like...him. He needed a disguise. She walked past him to his bedroom, and he followed her.

"Uh...what are you doing?" he asked, wide-eyed.

She stopped and looked up at him. "You can't go without a disguise. If my mom ever finds out who you are..." Her shoulders sagged, and she looked down. "You don't understand. For her, it's all about the money. The only reason she took me when my dad died was because he had set aside money for me and it was only given out a little at a time. If it hadn't been, she'd have taken the money and dumped me." Why had she said that last part? He didn't need to know that.

Instead of commenting on her sad tale, he went into his closet and moments later came back out. "How's this?"

She snickered. He looked ridiculous with his oversized sunglass and black felt fedora. He even had his shirt collar up.

"What?"

Sara shook her head and turned to leave the bedroom.

He caught up with her and turned her around. "What?"

She chewed the tip of her thumb. "Your disguise makes you look funny."

"Are you ready?" He was trying so hard not to smile, but the corners of his mouth were twitching.

They walked to the garage, got in the SUV, and she started it. "You know you don't have to wear that until we get into town."

He pulled off the hat and sunglasses. "Better?"

Oh yeah. What was her problem? A few more butterflies, and she'd practically be swooning. What was it about him? She needed to get a grip. She wasn't crossing the line beyond friendship. He was her client. It didn't matter how much she liked him. Plus, as long as her mom was on the loose, a relationship was out of the question.

"So, your mom. Where was she when your dad had you?" Liam asked as they rode to town.

She kept her eyes on the road. He already knew more than he should. Would the details really matter? "I don't know. It took them months to find her. When they did, she was ready to sign her rights away, until they told her I came with money. Then she was Mother of the Year. Until she got me home."

He touched her arm. "You don't have to answer my questions if you don't want to."

"You should be prepared. She's vicious when it comes to money. I've never met a more money-hungry person in my life...well, other than Chris." Why did she say that? Liam didn't need to know about him.

One eyebrow shot up. "Who's Chris?"

"Someone my mother got along famously with. I dated him about six months, and then he won a twenty-million-dollar lottery. There were already a few red flags beginning to pop up, but after he won, his personality changed dramatically." She glanced at him. "He's still friends with my mom. From time to time, he'll give her money." She needed this conversation to go the other direction. "How about you? Have you come closer to figuring out why you don't want to get out of your wheelchair?"

He rubbed his palms down his jeans and cleared his throat. "I think I'm scared I'll get hurt again. No one knows how much pain I was in when I woke up. It felt like I was broken in two. Every inch of me hurt to be touched. I don't want to go through that again."

That's what she'd figured, but telling him that would've only made him put up a wall. He had to come to it on his own. It was a battle only he could fight. "I can't imagine."

"Everyone wants me to get back out there like nothing happened, and in the world of football, it really was nothing. Only, there are times when I can still feel it. I'll dream about it and wake up in the middle of the night in a cold sweat. It terrifies me. Kimberly sacrificed so much so I could play, and I love football, but I don't want to play anymore." He covered his mouth with his hand, looking almost shocked he'd said it.

Sara stopped the car and put the brake on, turning to him. "And it's okay to feel like that. Anyone who doesn't respect your feelings doesn't need your love or your friendship. Kimberly sacrificed for you because she loves you and you love football. If you tell her what you just told me, she'll fight off anyone who tries to make you play."

He looked down. "You don't think she'll be disappointed in me?"

She tipped his chin up. "No. I don't think she will, and if she is, that's something she has to come to terms with. You can't play football when you don't want to. You'll get hurt again if you do."

Without a word, he pulled her into a hug and held her. It wasn't romantic in any way. It was more like

"Thank you for hearing me."

When her stomach growled, he let her go and laughed. "Guess we need to get those burgers." He smiled, and her stomach did little flips. Why did his smile have to be so great?

"I guess so." She put the SUV in drive and continued down the mountain. "So, tell me how you got into football."

She spent the rest of the ride to town learning about his childhood. His parents were killed in a car accident when he was twelve and his sister was eighteen. She'd taken him and raised him, sometimes working two jobs to support them. His family hadn't been wealthy. When his parents died, the only thing they got was the house.

It was fun listening to him talk, and she didn't have to talk about her mom or Chris. It was a win-win: learning about him and avoiding any questions.

THE BURGER and onion rings were just what Liam needed and, by the little moans, what Sara needed too. He was glad she was feeling better. "I never get tired of them."

She looked at him and shook her head. "No, they're amazing. I was starving."

"You should have had onions." He winked.

"I don't think my stomach could have handled them today." She wiped her mouth and wrapped up the rest of her burger. "I can't eat anymore. I think two days with no food put the kybosh on binge eating."

He shook his head. "You didn't even get onion rings."

She snagged a small one from his bag. "I didn't need any."

"Hey! I was going to eat that." He reached out to grab it, and she popped it in her mouth. "You little rat. You said you were full."

"I had room for one."

Her laughter was sweet, and she looked at him wide-eyed. When she finished it, she acted like she was going steal another one, and he batted at her hand. "I'm kidding. If you want one, take it."

"I don't. I just wanted to see what you'd do." She chuckled and looked out the window. "Oh no. She must have seen me the other day."

"Your mom's here?"

"Just pulled up. Lay the seat back and pull your coat over your head. Whatever happens, do not take that coat off." She looked at him, her eyebrows drawn together. "No matter what happens."

The look in her eyes screamed, *Danger!* so he pulled the coat over his head, wondering what could possibly happen. When Sara turned away from him, he angled the coat so he could peek through with one eye.

She rolled the window down as the woman stopped at the car. "Well, well, well, this is some SUV."

"It's just a car." Sara shrugged.

"And who's that in the seat?" her mom asked, peeking around Sara.

Shaking her head, Sara said, "He's my client, and I can't discuss him. He allowed me to stop for a bite to eat while he took a nap."

Like something out of a movie, her mom reached through the window and took Sara by the throat. "This is at least a $200,000 Mercedes. I should know. Husband number three had one. *Who* is your client?"

"No." Sara grabbed her mom's wrist and tried to pry her hand off. "Stop. I will not tell you anything. I promised to take care of him, and I will."

He saw the woman's fingers tighten around Sara's throat, and she struggled to breathe. "You shouldn't be so stubborn."

"We are in a public place. Everyone can see you, and all I have to do is hit the horn," Sara choked out.

"Didn't you promise to take care of me? Wouldn't that break your promise?" Her mom grinned. "Who is in the seat?"

"Never," Sara managed to strain out.

Those fingers on her throat clamped down so hard Sara could no longer breathe.

Liam was done. He started to move, and she pointed her finger at him again. How much abuse was she going to take to protect him? And how much was he willing to let her take to stay hidden?

She grabbed the key fob and hit the alarm button. The SUV lit up, and it blared. Sara's mother made a face and let her go with a shove and ran. Sara gulped for air and coughed.

He went to throw the coat off, but she pushed him down and rolled the window up. Then she collapsed back against the seat, holding her neck and sucking in air. Liam reached out to her, but she put up her hand.

"No, she's still watching." She turned in the seat to face him and drew her legs under her. "Stay down." Minutes ticked by before she could breathe normally again. "I'll get you out of here in a minute. We'll drive around for a while, and maybe I can keep her from following us. I shouldn't have brought you here. I should've known she saw me."

"I can handle myself, you know. I'm twice your size."

She leaned down and put her head on the center console. "My mom isn't someone to mess with. You don't know what she's capable of." With a deep breath, she sat up. "I can't let her hurt you, and she will."

He didn't know what to say. Never had he witnessed anything like that. "Do you know how hard it was to stay under that coat while she did that to you?"

"We'll go back to the house, and I won't leave until the job is over. I still won't tell her who you are, but at least I won't have access to you anymore and her dreams of whatever will be gone." Sara started the SUV and backed out.

Won't have access to him anymore? He didn't like that thought at all. No. He couldn't think that way. The last time he had thoughts like that, he'd nearly destroyed any kind of relationship with her. No, she would leave, and he'd go back to his life. She was his nurse, and he was her client. That was enough. Or was it?

CHAPTER 14

a couple days later, Liam eyed the phone sitting on his nightstand. Kimberly was on her honeymoon, but he wanted to talk to her so bad. It was a little after eight in the morning, and he was tired of wheeling himself around in a wheelchair in public.

His only hesitation was Sara. He didn't want her to leave yet. They had two days left. Then again, Kim liked Sara. Maybe if he told her he liked her, he could convince her to extend her honeymoon and Sara's employment.

Grabbing the phone, he hit her number before he could chicken out.

"Liam? Is everything okay? Where's Sara?" The noise in the background made it hard to hear.

"Whoa, Kim, everything's fine. I'm calling because I

145

need to talk to you and it can't wait." He sat down hard on his bed and flopped on his back. "Are you some-where you can sit down and talk?"

"Hold on." The noise died, and Kim came back on the phone. "Yeah, what do you need to talk about?"

"I've been pretending to still be hurt."

"I kinda knew, little brother."

"Yeah, but you don't know why."

"Then why?"

He sat up and raked his hand through his hair. "I don't want to play football anymore."

"What? Why?"

Admitting he was scared was hard. He was over six feet tall, built like a tank, and had an attitude to go with it most of the time. It was the truth, though. "I'm scared to. Kim, every time I think about going back out there, I panic. I can't. At least, not yet."

"Why didn't you say that?"

"I thought you'd be disappointed in me. You sacri-ficed a lot so I could be a football player, and I don't want you to think I didn't appreciate it."

A little laugh. "I don't think that at all. The only reason I wanted you to play is because you loved it. If you don't want to play anymore, you aren't going to get an argument from me. Every time you went out there, my heart was in my throat."

"Really?"

"Yeah, I didn't want you to get hurt, and then you did. If you never touch another football, I will be just fine."

If he'd known it'd be that easy, he'd have come clean months ago. "I had no idea."

"Seems neither of us was listening to the other."

He grunted. "Seems so."

"I guess I can get Sara out of your hair, huh?"

"No." He'd said it too quickly.

"Oh, really?" Kim was grinning ear to ear. He could see it in his mind.

"I like her, but I don't know if it's like that. I'm not ready for her to go." Beyond that, he was confused as all get out. One minute he was wanting to kiss her until he couldn't breathe, and the next, he was wondering if he could build an actual wall to keep them firmly in the friend category.

"You've got two days to figure it out." She laughed.

"That's the thing."

"Okay, what?"

"I'll pay for you to stay another week on your honeymoon if you'll call Sara and ask her to stay another week."

Kim didn't just laugh, she cackled. "Oh, baby brother, I do love you, and I really like Sara. If there's a chance something's there, I'll stay here as long as you want me to."

"You will?"

"Yeah, if you have a chance to be happy with a real woman, you bet."

He rolled his eyes. "Models are real women, Kim."

"Yes, and some of them have been really sweet, but you want more than that. Sara is different. She's funny, insightful, sweet...and the little bit I've talked with her, she's not the kind of woman who comes along very often."

Well, Kim was right about that. Sara was not cookie-cutter, for sure. "No, she's not. I don't know if I'm ready for anything more than friendship, but I do have feelings for her. If she leaves..."

"I'll call her right now. I'll even beg if I have to."

He did a fist pump and smiled. "Thanks. You're doing it right now?"

"Yeah."

"I love you, Kim."

"I love you too."

He ended the call, lighter than he'd felt in the past year. Telling his sister the truth more than set him free. It was like he could take a deep breath for the first time since he was hurt.

If Kim was calling Sara, he wanted to hear it.

Would it really be wrong to listen in? It was worth the risk. Kicking his shoes off, he walked out of his room, and when he got close to Sara's room, he slowed down. The door was open barely a sliver, just enough that he could hear what was being said.

"Really?"

He took a chance and looked in the door. Sara was folding clothes, and she had the phone on speaker.

"Another week?"

"Yeah, it was a surprise. He knew how much I was enjoying it and just let me know today. Is it too last minute to get you to stay another week?"

Sara dropped her arms and stared at the phone. "Uh, I'd love to stay, but I don't think he's going to like that."

What? What gave her that idea? He stopped himself before he actually burst into the room and asked her.

"Kimberly, as much as I'd like to stay, he needs his space. He's trapped in that wheelchair, and he's used to being free. I know you love him, but—"

"I only need another week. When I get back, I'll talk to him, but I'm out of the country. What if something happened and I wasn't able to get there on time?"

Sara's shoulders sagged, and she pressed her hand to her forehead. "Yeah, I know. I'll stay."

"I'm sorry. I know he can be a real pill."

Sara picked up the phone and took it off speaker, putting it to her ear. "Actually, he's been really sweet. I've enjoyed spending time with him."

Liam's lips spread into a grin so wide his face hurt.

"I don't know about that."

What he wouldn't give to know what Kim was saying. Maybe he'd call her and ask. He leaned his shoulder against the wall and continued listening.

Sara laughed. "I do really like him."

"Feelings? Well, I don't know. He's my client."

"No, I wouldn't."

Wouldn't what? What wouldn't she do? It was killing him, only hearing one side of the conversation.

"He does?"

He does what? Liam rubbed his face with his hands in frustration.

"No."

Why did she have to take the phone off of speaker? He tapped his forehead. This was the punishment for eavesdropping; he was sure of it.

"Okay, are you going to tell him?"

"Me?"

"Okay, I'll tell him. I just hope he doesn't flip."

"Have fun, Kimberly. Bye."

SARA SET HER PHONE DOWN. Kimberly was out of her mind. Liam didn't have feelings for her. Sure, they were getting along, but getting along didn't translate into actual feelings. Why had Kim even thought that? Pushing the crazy thought aside, Sara concentrated on the bigger issue at hand.

How was she going to tell Liam she was staying another week? His sister needed to back off. She stood and walked to the door, pausing to gather her courage. They'd been getting along, but she was supposed to be leaving in two days.

What would happen when he found out she was staying another week? Would he start treating her badly again? He promised he wouldn't, but she'd found most people never kept their promises, which is why she worked so hard to keep hers.

There was no point in waiting, she walked out the door and down the hall to the living room. "Liam?"

He walked out of his room and looked at her funny. "Everything okay?"

"Uh, well," she said and tucked a piece of her hair behind her ear. "I got a call from Kimberly just now."

Liam's face fell. Oh great. He was going to be so upset.

"She…"

He walked to her and stopped. "She what?"

"She wants me to stay another week. I'm sorry."

His eyes held hers. "Why?" The frustration was evident in his tone.

"William surprised her with an extended honeymoon. I tried to get out of it, but she's worried because she's out of the country. She said she'll talk to you when she gets back." She hated doing it to him. It cut her to the core. He was desperate for space.

Raking his hand through his hair, he walked to the couch and sat down. "I know she's out of the country, but I wish she'd have talked to me first."

She followed him to the couch and sat down beside him. "Yeah, I wish she had too. I'm so sorry." She touched his knee and hung her head. "I can stay in my room if you'd like. I know you don't need my help, so it's silly to have me around."

"No, that's stupid. We'll keep things status quo."

Her heart was breaking for him. She wished there was something she could do. "You could call her and tell her the truth. Then you'd be rid of me."

"Not yet."

Something in the way he said it made her take another look at him, but she nodded. If he wasn't ready, he wasn't ready. No one could force people to do things before they were ready, especially people who'd suffered trauma. "Okay."

He looked at her and scrunched up his nose. "I do have that gala thing in California. Would you want to go with me?"

Her eyebrows scrunched together. "You'd have to take your wheelchair. Aren't you sick of it?"

"I'm not taking it. I'm done pretending."

"You are?"

He nodded. "Yeah. Besides, if we go, I'd like to be able to dance with you."

"But won't Kimberly be upset if you don't tell her first?"

"She's on her honeymoon. I'll tell her when she gets back."

Sara chewed her thumb. "I don't know. You could really hurt her."

"I kinda need to go. I'm one of the people being honored." He said it like he was ashamed.

Sara tilted her head. "Honored for what?"

"I kinda donated to this school in a little town in South Africa. Or, well, had the school built. I have a friend who works with Doctors Without Borders, and he said the kids there needed it. So, I...gave them the money. I didn't really expect—"

She flung herself at him and hugged him. "I worked

with them right out of school. You have no idea what that means to those small villages. The children will have hot meals and an education. It means getting out of poverty." She pulled back and kissed him. Her eyes widened, and she scrambled away, taking a seat in one of the armchairs. "I am so, so sorry."

What was her deal? Kissing him? She'd been so out of sorts since she started the job. What had gotten into her? *A beautiful man with gorgeous red hair and a killer smile. Duh*, her heart said.

"It's okay. I think I prefer being kissed more than the award. It seems kind of stupid. Rewarding people for being good people. Why would you do that? Isn't it supposed to be because you want to and not because of some award?"

"Do you really want to go, then?"

He shrugged. "Yeah, because my friend should be there. I don't get to see him much because he's out of the country a lot."

"I would love to go with you, but I don't have anything to wear for a gala. I don't even know *what* to wear to something like that. Katarina was right. I really don't fit in your world. I never will." Not with her convict, scam-artist mom.

Liam shot her a smile. "If you want to go, we'll find you a dress. I would like you to come with me. Can't really take care of me if you're here in Denver and I'm in California."

Oh boy. When he put it like that, what was she supposed to do? "Okay."

"Great."

Yeah, great. Hobnobbing with people wealthy enough to provide small villages with schools. She'd stick out like a sore thumb with gangrene. If she kept quiet and watched herself, maybe she could go unnoticed.

CHAPTER 15

*S*ara walked out of the bathroom, toweling her hair. Liam had gone into town without her, and it was making her a nervous wreck. If something happened to him and she wasn't around, she'd never forgive herself. Her mother had pretty much guaranteed she'd be confined to the house after their last encounter.

She'd spent the evening before online, looking at dresses and picking a few out to try on at the house. If felt so strange to be looking at dresses so expensive they could pay a month's rent, but there were expectations at things like galas. Even the word sounded fancy. Gala. Ga. La.

He'd taken the wheelchair with him to keep up pretenses, but he'd taken a different car. The area of town he'd be in wasn't exactly where her mom frequented, so Sara had high hopes he'd be able to get there and back without being seen.

She sat on the edge of the bed and rubbed her temple. The moment of shock where she realized she'd kissed him came roaring back. If she was honest, she'd wanted to kiss him again, but that was a bad line to cross.

Whatever it took, she had to stop thinking about him. But as much as she didn't want to admit, she had feelings for him. He'd done something so amazing it had given her goosebumps. He was funny and charming; not to mention attractive. That red hair of his was killing her. Then add that little freckle above his lip, and it was all she could do to keep her lips to herself.

Sara needed something to do before she thought herself into the crazy house. She stood and walked out to the living room, stopping at the front window overlooking the driveway.

She crossed her arms over her chest. Goosey was sitting at the end of the driveway, and if she remembered right, there was a book somewhere in the seats. Her gaze roamed over the front of the lawn. It was snowy, but it was winter in Denver and she was on the side of a mountain.

It wasn't that far to the car. If she ran, she could

grab the book and be back in less than five minutes. The fire would feel great after being in the brisk, cool morning. It'd wake her up so the heat and the book could slowly lull her back to sleep.

For a second, she contemplated getting her coat. Did she really need it for a quick in and out? She'd done that plenty of times. Her keys were in the pocket, but she hadn't locked the doors. Who would steal Goosey, especially at the top of the mountain? A deep breath, and she was out the door, hustling down the steps and crossing the driveway to her car.

The door hinges screeched as she opened it. Goosey didn't like winter. Never had. Sara rubbed her arms and crawled into the passenger seat. More than likely, the book was wedged between the driver's seat and the door, or under the seat. She stretched across the bench seat and slid her hand down, feeling around. Nothing. Then she climbed over the seat, into the back seat, and looked under them.

Her book was in there; she knew it. She flopped back over, into the passenger seat, and hit it hard. The car rocked back, and she jerked her attention to the parking brake. "Oh, no." Goosey didn't have her emergency brake on. Her brakes were okay, but she needed the little boost the brake gave her.

Pavement crunched under the wheels as the old car

slowly rolled back. "No, no, no, no, no." Tears were already pooling in her eyes. She couldn't lose one of the few things she had left of her dad.

Sara scooted into the driver's seat and pushed her foot down hard on the emergency brake. It wasn't working, and Goosey was rolling faster. A glance over her shoulder, and her eyes widened. The car would be going over the side of the mountain in mere minutes. If only she hadn't left her coat with her keys in the house!

She quickly stood and tried to stop the car from rolling, but the metal monster was too heavy. It knocked her down, and as she fell, her shirt caught on the door. Now it was dragging her along.

If she didn't get free, she and Goosey were going to do their own version of *Thelma and Louise*. Her side was burning, her cheek hurt, and it was getting hard to think. There was no way to save her dad's car, so she poked her finger through the hole the door had made in her shirt and ripped it from the door.

As she stood, she wobbled, and the car careened over the side of the mountain. She ran to the edge and watched as it tumbled, front over end until it slid to a stop. It wasn't like the movies. There was no large explosion, but Goosey sure was dead. Why hadn't she put the parking brake on to begin with? Would it have mattered? She'd punched them and nothing had happened.

Her mom was right. She was an idiot. She rubbed her arms as she hugged herself, mourning the loss of her car, and then she trudged back to the house. It took effort to keep walking and even more to climb the stairs. By the time she walked in the door, she wondered how she'd made it back to the house.

THE FIRST THING Liam noticed as he returned to the house was that Sara's car was missing. He'd gone to town without her because she didn't want her mom to see her. Why would her car be gone?

He pulled into the garage and pulled out his tuxedo and a few of the dresses she'd picked out. It was cute, watching her expression the previous evening when she was looking at them online. The little "o" her mouth would make and how her eyes would grow large when she saw the price were adorable.

What he really liked about her was that she'd fought for him. After seeing the sadness in her eyes when she was telling him about Kimberly's call, he'd almost broken down and told her the truth. The pout on her lips. The way she was looking at him. It was killer.

It had taken him forever to fall asleep. Between being elated she was staying and then picturing her dressed up, his mind was all over the place. She may not think she belonged in his world, but he had no doubt she did.

The confusion was still there. Did he want a relationship? If he did, was he really looking for one that was long term? Sara was long term. She was forever. Was he ready for that? He'd already made so many mistakes, and they weren't even dating. They'd just managed to become friends.

Pushing through the door, he walked through the mudroom and into the kitchen, to find her standing at the front door with her forehead leaned against it. "Sara?" If she was in the house, where was her car?

She lifted her head and turned. Blood trickled down her right temple, her jaw and cheek were scratched, and her shirt was nearly ripped in half.

His heart hit the floor, along with everything he was carrying. Time slowed, and for a split second, he was paralyzed. The car was missing, and she was injured. Oh, this wasn't good.

He strode from the kitchen and stopped in front of her "What happened?"

162

She blinked, and he wondered if she could even register what he was saying. "I lost Goosey."

"What do you mean you 'lost Goosey'?"

Sara looked up at him, and her eyes were glassy. "I was getting a book, and she started rolling back. I tried to stop her. The brakes wouldn't work. She was going so fast, and she was so heavy. I tried to press the emergency brake, but it wouldn't work."

She wobbled, and he took her arms to steady her. Her hands wrapped around his biceps, looking like she'd been hit with a stun gun.

"When I tried to stop her, my shirt got caught. She was dragging me." She looked down at her clothes. "I had to tear it." She looked back up, and his breath caught. Her eyes were filled with tears. "She was all I had left of him. I had eight years where someone loved me, really loved me. My dad loved me. He took care of me. He would tell me I was pretty. Brush my hair. He would read to me and tell me I was smart. She's all I had left of him, and she just fell down the side of a mountain."

The lump in his throat grew. He had no idea the grief she must be experiencing. "I'm so sorry." That car meant everything to her. It was big and ugly, but she loved it.

She touched her forehead to his chest. "She was

going to pull me with her. I had to let her go. I had to. Why did she have to go?"

Her knees buckled, and he put his arm around her. She cried out, so he moved his arm. Road rash covered her side and hip. Her thin little pajamas pants were shredded.

"I don't think I have any internal damage, but I may have hit my head." She touched it and then looked at her hand. "I'm bleeding. I may need to go to the emergency room."

"I agree."

Her head fell back as she went limp, and he scooped her up. The car had fallen down the mountain and nearly dragged her along with it. He'd nearly lost her. The thought hit him in the chest. Life without Sara. Now that he knew what life was like with her, he didn't like what it would look like without her.

CHAPTER 16

$\mathscr{A}$side from the machines, it was so quiet that Liam's ears were ringing. The moment Sara went limp in his arms, he got her in the car and took off for the emergency room. At least he'd come clean to Kimberly. If anyone saw him walking around, she wouldn't be blindsided.

He sat facing Sara, holding her hand. It'd been six hours since he'd brought her in, and she'd yet to wake up. Her cheek and jaw were scratched up. She must have had enough wits to pick her face up; otherwise, they would be matching her side and hip, which had looked pretty raw from what little he'd overheard from the nurses.

That was her worst injury, which he'd also overheard. She'd have a scar there. They wouldn't really tell him anything because they didn't have permission to talk to him. It was incredibly frustrating, but they had laws and rules to follow, so he kept his temper in check.

They'd called her mom, and she hadn't shown up. He almost hoped she wouldn't. She was terrible to Sara. If he had his way, she'd never see her again. And if she did and she put her hands on her, they'd have words.

The physical injuries weren't nearly as significant as the emotional one. He'd never seen her look so lost when she was telling him what happened. The car her dad had given her was gone, and if she'd had a clearer head, he was sure she would've been on the verge of a breakdown.

Sara blinked and stirred. "Hi."

"Hey." He smiled and leaned across her, bracing his hand on the bed. "You sure your car isn't named *Christine?*"

She chuckled. "I'm sure." Then she pulled on his shirt like she was trying to pull him down. He leaned in, and she slipped her hand around his neck, pulling him further down, and touched her cheek to his. "Are you okay?"

Whoa. How could something so innocent feel like

so much more? "I should be asking you that." He pulled back and held her gaze.

"I promised to take care of you."

He smiled. "I feel very taken care of. How about that?"

She nodded as her eyes watered. "Goosey's gone."

"Yeah, she is. I'm so sorry." He wiped his thumb across her cheek and dried her tears. Maybe he could get the car back. It wasn't like he didn't have the money. Until he found out if it was possible, he'd keep the idea to himself. He didn't want to get her hopes up and then find out it wasn't.

She touched her fingers to her mouth, and her voice broke as she said, "I should have had her brakes checked when I was in town, but I wasn't feeling good."

"And you were upset with me." He would shoulder his part in it.

"Yeah, I was. I should have had a clearer head. I don't know what's wrong with me." She moved, and her face scrunched up. "Oh, that hurts."

"Road rash is all I know. I did hear someone say they wanted to keep you overnight for observation since you hit your head." He wanted so badly to hold her and kiss her. To take her hurt away. "They called your mom, by the way."

She nodded, and then her eyes widened as she seemed to realize what he'd said. "Liam, you have to go. You have to go now. My mom can't find you here."

"You said my name." He didn't even hear the rest of it. His name came from her lips, and he liked the sound of it.

"I'm sorry. My head hurts."

He smiled. "I've wanted you to call me Liam for a week now."

She grabbed his hand. "You still have to go. My mom will hurt you. She doesn't just marry men and take their money. She does anything she can to get money: blackmail, you name it."

"Why haven't you called the police?"

She shook her head and shrugged. "She's my mom. I thought maybe one day she'd decide she loved me and stop, but she doesn't and she's not." Sara grunted and sat up. "You have to go. Use the back exits; whatever you need to do. Don't let her see you. She's smart, and she'll put it together. Please go."

Liam leaned down and put a finger to her lips. "She choked you. I'm not leaving."

Sara pushed his finger aside. "This is the only way I can take care of you. If you don't go, I'll be breaking my promise."

"There's nothing she can do to me." He wasn't leaving. Her mom could try whatever she wanted. His lawyer was the best, and he didn't have anything to hide.

She took his face in her hands. "How about Kimberly? William? Your friends? It's not just you. You're the golden ticket she's been salivating for, and she *will* hurt you. She'll use anything she can to get what she wants."

He hadn't thought about that. Still, he wasn't leaving her. "Despite my reluctance to play football, I'm not a coward."

"I don't think that at all." She looked down and palmed her temple. "I...care what happens to you." Tears pooled in her eyes as she looked up. "You *have* to go."

None of it was sitting right with him. Running away? Leaving her alone with someone who'd strangled her? "Do you have any idea what you're asking me to do? I'd be abandoning you to save my own hide."

"No, you'd be helping me keep my promise to your sister. I'll be here another day, if that, and I'll be back. I won't be very fast, but I'll be back. Go. And don't return."

He slipped his arms around her and pulled her to him. "I don't like this. I don't want to do it."

"I know, but you will. I'll be fine."

Liam pulled back. "What's your definition of fine?"

A small smile played on her lips. "Not alone."

He chuckled and stood. "I hate this."

"I'll see you tomorrow. Stay home. Don't do anything stupid. At least not until I get back."

Instead of a smart comeback, he bent down and kissed her. He shouldn't have, but he couldn't stop himself. "Call me, and I'll send a car."

He walked to the door and glanced at her over his shoulder. Her eyes were huge, and her cheeks were tinted red. Then he winked and left. He was in trouble. He was looking at a downhill slope covered in oil. Forever was big, but it didn't seem so bad when he pictured her next to him.

HE KISSED HER? The conversation with Kim came rushing back. Did Liam have feelings for her? It was just a peck on the lips. More like the punctuation on the end of a sentence. It couldn't mean anything. Someone like Liam had probably done that plenty of times. It was just a show of care and friendship.

No matter what it could have meant, she *would* have to put a stop to the kissing. Not that she really wanted to, but they shouldn't and couldn't cross that line. It'd been hours since he'd left, and Sara had repeated that so many times it was like she was playing a skipping record.

So far, her mom hadn't shown up. It made her wish she hadn't made him leave. She didn't want him to. What she wanted was to crawl onto his lap and let him put his huge arms around her. Oh, she was falling hard for him.

What was going on with her? She'd never developed feelings for a client before. Granted, her youngest patient had been nine, and the next youngest had been sixty-eight. Still, she'd maintained a comfortable distance.

She rubbed her arms as she rolled her head and looked out the window. It was well past midnight, and for the life of her, she couldn't sleep. Her head still hurt a little. She hadn't hit it super hard. The blood on her temple was from a scratch caused by being pulled on the pavement.

The door handle jiggled, and Sara assumed it was a nurse coming in to do their blood pressure routine. Nope. It was her mother. Why didn't it surprise her that she was coming so late? What was she up to now?

Her mom grinned, and in behind her walked Chris. Fear stretched out an icy finger and played her spine like a harp. Didn't he know she had a restraining order on him? What was he doing in her room? She quietly slipped her fingers around the emergency button. If he tried anything, she'd be ready. The last time he'd come around, she'd acted too quickly, and he'd left before actually doing anything that could get him into trouble. Sara wasn't jumping the gun this time, and this time the little camera in the corner would catch him.

"I have a restraining order on you. There are cameras all over this hospital. You'll go to jail." She didn't beat around the bush. Not this time.

His lips curled into a snarl, and her mom stopped him as he lunged forward. He wasn't much taller than Sara, but he was built like a tank. If he wanted to hurt her, he could.

"Chris, you wouldn't want to do anything stupid. You're just here for…visual effect." Her mom smiled and stopped next to her bed.

"What do you want, Mom? I'm not giving you the name of my client. I'm not working for him anymore anyway, so I don't even have access to him now." She hoped she could sell the lie. Her original contract *was* up.

Her mother tilted her head. "See, that's where I think you're wrong. I think you have feelings for him, and something's telling me it's not one-sided. I wonder what he'd do to make sure you're okay."

Sara was frozen. Liam didn't think of her like that. Yeah, he'd kissed her, but it wasn't romantic, no matter how much she wanted it to be. "No, he doesn't. I don't get involved with my clients, ever. I have a signed confidentiality agreement. I can't tell you his name or anything about him. If I do, I'll be sued. I need the money from this job to pay the rent until my next job."

Chris stepped behind her mom. "I think you need to waggle your tongue a little."

"You have millions. Why would you be involved in this?" For the life of her, she couldn't understand what was going on. What was he doing, hanging around with her mom?

"I made a few bad investments."

Her jaw dropped. "All that money is gone already? How is that even possible?"

This time her mom couldn't stop him, and he grabbed her by the throat. Sara pressed the button and hoped he wouldn't snap her neck before someone came in. "You have a smart-mouth."

"I will not tell you," she choked out.

Chris squeezed a little harder and growled.

Her mom pulled his hand off. "Look, that's not going to get us what we want. I'm telling you; they've got something going on."

Sara held her throat and coughed. "If you go after

him in any way, I'll be done protecting you," she wheezed.

"And break your promise? Hardly." She crossed her arms over her chest. "I know how precious those promises are to you."

For the first time, she found herself hating her mom. Why did it have to be this way? "What happened to you to make you this way? Why do you have to be like this?"

She lifted a solitary eyebrow. "Let's just say not everyone has a charmed life like you."

Charmed? "I took care of you, starting when I was eight. You would go out, be gone for days, and come home drunk. You have called me all sorts of horrible names, manipulated me, and treated me like dirt. If that's a charmed life, you have a warped perception of charmed."

One side of her lip curled up. "I took your smart butt in when no one else wanted you."

Something in Sara snapped. She'd dealt with this thing resembling a human being for twenty years, and suddenly, she was done holding it in. "Yeah, because I came with money. You didn't take me in; you took my dad's money and blew it on booze. When you weren't running a con job, we lived in filth. It took me getting a job when I was sixteen to finally have a clean place to sleep."

The door opened, and a nurse walked in. "May I help you?"

Sara smiled as she glared at her mom. "Yes, these two people need to be escorted out. I have a restraining order on him, and she's not related to me."

Chris paled and clipped the nurse on the shoulder as he ran out of the room.

Her mom pointed a finger in her face. "I'll get what I want. You mark my word."

It took work, but Sara slipped off the bed and stood. "You go near him, and I'll have a police report filed so fast you'll get whiplash. I'm done taking care of you. This is one promise it won't hurt me to break." She clenched her jaw. "I'm done with you. Your name isn't on my lease, and I'm calling the landlord and paying to have the locks changed."

Regina nearly growled, but before she could touch Sara, security walked in. "I'll get you for this. You just wait. I'm not done with you." Her screams echoed through the hospital and got fainter the further security took her.

With her mom gone, and the adrenaline quickly wearing off, Sara's surge of energy was fading fast. The nurse grabbed her as her knees buckled and helped her get back into bed. Her entire body ached, and her hip burned like fire.

"I'm so sorry for all the chaos," Sara said.

The woman smiled and patted her hand. "It's taken care of. They won't be coming back. The police have been called, and they'll be taking a statement in a little while, okay? For now, you need to rest."

Rest. It sounded great. Her eyes closed, and she mumbled, "Thanks." Her mind was muddy, and all she could think was that she wanted Liam back. "Call Liam. Please. Liam Thomas." And everything became a blur.

CHAPTER 17

*H*earing Liam's voice made Sara smile. She knew he wasn't with her, but the dream she had sure made it feel real. Sunlight filtered through the window and nearly blinded her as she opened her eyes. Her late-night scuffle with her mom had worn her out.

As her head cleared, she realized Liam was standing in her room, talking to two police officers. He'd come back? Now her mom would know who he was. Why did he do that?

"Mr. Thomas, what are you doing here?" She was furious. He said he'd stay away. How could she protect him if he wouldn't listen?

He leveled his eyes at her like he was annoyed she'd used his last name. "The hospital called when your emergency contact was escorted off the property and you asked them to call me."

She didn't remember that. "Oh, I did?"

He nodded. "These two police officers would like to talk to you." He crossed his arms over his chest. "You should tell them everything."

Now that the police were here, her courage was waning a little. Breaking her promise made her stomach drop. She knew she needed to do it, but it didn't make it any easier.

"I've already told them what happened at Greasy Burger."

For a split second, anger surged through her, and just as quickly as it had come, it was gone. Liam was right. This wasn't breaking her promise; this was keeping it. If Regina wasn't stopped, one day someone would get angry and hurt her mother. "I'm ready."

The police officers walked to the end of the bed and began asking her question after question.

Sara started from the beginning, when her mom first took custody of her, telling them everything. Well, minus the part where her mom was convinced Liam had feelings for her. Or that she had feelings for him. Why had she waited so long to let authorities know about Regina?

"And that's all?" one of the officers asked.

She nodded. "Yes."

The second officer put his hand over the gun on his hip. "And you don't know where she is currently?"

"No, she was taken out of here by security, and I told her she couldn't stay with me anymore." Didn't mean she wouldn't go back to the apartment and trash it, but Sara was done sharing with her mother.

"Those bruises on your neck; did she do those?" the second officer asked.

Sara looked down and wrung her hands. She didn't want to say anything in front of Liam, but she really didn't have a choice. "No, those are from my ex-boyfriend, Chris Burdine. I have a restraining order on him. The moment the nurse showed up, he ran off."

Liam sat beside her. "He put his hands on you?" The question came out like a growl.

She looked up at him. "Yeah. He has a bad temper. It's why I broke up with him."

The police officer looked over the notes they'd taken and then looked at her. "Okay. If we need anything else, we'll give you a call."

"Okay."

The moment the officers were out the door, Liam caught her gaze and held it. "If he ever puts his hands on you again, you won't need a restraining order any more."

"Stop. He's not worth it. He blew all that money, and now he's hustling with my mom. I'm so done."

He leaned across her and braced his hand on the bed. "And don't call me Mr. Thomas again."

Sara looked away. "I was mad. You weren't supposed to come back."

He took her chin and made her look at him. "Hey, the hospital calls and says something's happened and you're asking for me. What can I do?"

"I don't remember that." She tried so hard not to smile, but it spread on her lips against her will. "And you tell them no."

Liam shook his head. "I don't think so." He paused as his gaze roamed over her face. "Are you okay?"

How did she answer that? She'd lost Goosey, broken her promise to her mom, and more than likely broken her promise to Kimberly. Add to that, she was falling for him. "I don't know." It was her best answer at the moment. Her ability to process felt broken.

"Your mom is in some pretty big trouble. Why are you willing to break your promise now? What happened to make you do that?" Liam asked.

Her heart sped up as he stared at her. She shrugged. "It was time."

He narrowed his eyes. "It's been time. Why now?"

"Regina said she'd come after you. I had to choose."

Why did she say that? She should have said it was because she was tired of dealing with her. It was the truth, and coupled with the idea that she'd go after Liam, that was the last straw.

A small smile grew on his lips. "And you chose me? Why?"

Why was he making this so hard? She paused while she tried to think of something, and then it hit her. "Lesser of two evils."

He threw his head back and laughed. "Smart-mouth."

"You asked."

Drawing closer, he cupped her face, and it felt like all the air had been sucked out of the room. His lips parted as he pressed them to her cheek, brushed them down her face, and rested his mouth against her ear. "They called and said you'd been assaulted. It felt like I was driving in wet cement the entire way here. I'm not leaving this hospital again without you."

Her heart was beating so hard she could hear the blood rushing in her ears. What if her mom was right? What if he did have feelings for her? He was a client. She couldn't get involved with him.

The questions and doubts didn't stop her from leaning into him. His warmth and comfort were like a lighthouse, and she felt like a ship that had been lost at sea for years, desperate for hope and home.

She couldn't think that way. If her mom got anything to back up her suspicion, he'd get hurt. Her mom wouldn't care who she used to do it either. Even if Sara wanted something with him, it would never work. Not with her mom lurking around. If she cared anything about him at all, at the end of the week, she'd walk away and never look back.

But in the meantime, she could soak him up. Enjoy his company, his security, and his warmth. She wrapped her arms around his neck and buried her hands in his hair. "Thank you for coming."

Liam pulled back and pressed his forehead to hers. "Anytime."

Oh, she was in big, big trouble.

LIAM LET his gaze roam over Sara's face as she slept in his arms with her head tipped back like she was looking at him. He'd spent the previous restless night thinking of nothing but what it looked like that he'd taken off. He should have stayed firm and stayed at the hospital. It was the second time he'd listened to her, and there wouldn't be a third. Not when it came to her mother. He understood her fear, even admired her conviction in keeping her promises, but he wasn't playing the part of a coward again.

What would have happened if she hadn't been quick enough to call a nurse? If he ever got his hands on the so-called man she'd dated, he wouldn't be walking again anytime soon.

How could a man put his hands on a woman like that? It baffled him. Really, it baffled him that anyone could raise their fist to another human being just because they wanted to. Self-defense, sure; but not just to hurt someone.

He caressed her cheek with his fingertips. She smiled and snuggled closer, stretching her arm across his chest. Is this what it'd be like to be with her? To drift to sleep, wrapped up in her? She said her dad had been the only one to ever really love her, and he couldn't fathom that.

This beautiful woman had a depth he'd never come across before. She could make him laugh like no other. Her smile lit his blood on fire. He…he loved her. The thought made him pause, but it was as clear as any feeling he'd ever had. He loved everything about her. Forever with her could work. He would make it work. But would she?

He was her client. She'd been clear she couldn't

cross that line. There'd been nothing from her to indicate she thought about him the same way. Yeah, she'd flirted and kissed him twice, and he was pretty sure she liked him. But that didn't mean she had feelings for him. At least, not equal to his. What if she didn't, and it was all one-sided?

She opened her eyes and smiled. "Why are you staring at me?"

That was easy. "Because you're beautiful."

A small shake of her head. "Right. The left side of my face looks like it's been chewed on."

He held her gaze. "Your beauty is not defined by your looks, Sara Lynch. Don't get me wrong; you are drop-dead gorgeous. I thought that from day one. But your beauty comes from so deep inside that it would take more than a few scratches to even come close to dulling it."

The tips of her ears turned red, and she broke eye contact. "That's the nicest thing anyone has ever said to me. I don't know how to respond other than thank you."

Lifting her chin with his finger, he grinned. "You could kiss me."

"I don't think..." She stopped mid-sentence and held his gaze a moment. Then she slipped her hand behind his neck and brought his lips down to hers.

The light touch of her lips caused stars to explode behind his eyes.

He pressed the flat of his hand against the middle of her back to pull her closer and buried his hands in her hair. Their lips moved together, and all he could think was she was what he wanted.

She broke the kiss with a groan, and punctuating each word with feathery kisses, she said, "This is a bad idea. I shouldn't be kissing you."

With the last touch of her lips, he cupped her head and deepened the kiss. She circled her arm around his neck and threaded her fingers through his hair. He couldn't get enough of her. She was better than anything he'd ever had. There wasn't a wine made that could beat the sweetness of her lips or the dizzying effect she had on him.

A rattling of the door handle, and they broke apart, flushed and breathing hard.

A nurse walked in and smiled. "I'm just checking on you, seeing if you're okay. Need to get your blood pressure really quick, and I'll be out."

"That's one test I'm going to fail," she muttered.

Liam snorted and looked away. Yeah, he was glad they weren't checking his. He was sure his was in the stratosphere. After three tries and more than a few confused looks, the nurse left.

"I'm not opposed to picking up where we left off," Liam said and chuckled.

Sara shook her head and chewed her thumb. "I don't know. You're my client. I shouldn't have done that."

The way she said it made him reluctant to push the issue. How could he get her to change her mind? To see things a different way? What if he could keep her close and show her they could make it work? He had a week left. They still had the gala in California to go to. They could fly out a day early, see the sites, and spend time together. If she'd go for it or felt up to it. He'd wait a couple days and see how she was doing, and then they'd do something spontaneous. Or spontaneous for her. He'd have it set up already in case she was able to go.

She covered her mouth as she yawned. "I'm sorry. I'm tired, but I'm hurting."

Liam pressed the call-nurse button, and a nurse replied. "Sara Lynch needs something for pain. She's unable to sleep."

The nurse called back, "Someone will be there in a moment."

Her mouth dropped open. "Why'd you do that?"

"You said you're hurting."

"But I can handle it." She pinched her lips together.

A nurse walked in, holding a syringe, and stopped at the bed. "I hear you're having trouble sleeping."

Sara blinked. "That was fast."

In seconds, the nurse was done and gone, and Sara's eyes were already getting droopy.

"Feeling better?"

She nodded. "And sleepy," she said and threw her legs over his.

He pulled her on top of him, and she laid her head on his chest. "Better?"

A slow exhale, and she melted into him. "I like it when you hold me."

Oh, whatever they'd given her was good stuff. "Oh yeah?"

Sara nodded. "I feel safe. I don't feel safe very much."

He combed his fingers down the length of her hair. "You're safe with me. I won't let anyone hurt you." And he wasn't going to hurt her again either. "I promise." He'd make good on it too.

She lifted up and stared at him. Her head tilted, and her glazed-over eyes roamed over his face.

"What?"

Without a word, she pulled herself up and kissed him. Then she laid her head on his shoulder. "I like your freckle."

Before he could come up with a smart comeback, she was out. He pushed her hair back from her face and held it. Man, he loved her. He'd never thought those words about a woman, much less felt them. Sara Lynch had his heart. She could have all his freckles if she wanted.

CHAPTER 18

*I*t'd been three days since Sara returned to Liam's home. He'd been a bit of a pest, and now she had a deeper appreciation for what her clients must go through. Although, she did kind of like it. He'd lay down with her and hold her, and it was the best feeling in the world.

Using the wall, she braced her hand against it as she entered the living room. She was still pretty sore, but the more she walked, the better she felt.

"What are you doing?" Liam asked.

Great. "I'm walking."

"You're supposed to take it easy." He crossed the room so fast he was almost a blur.

He'd been super sweet, but he was doing her job. She was supposed to be taking care of him. "I need to move around. It's the only way to work the soreness out."

His arm slid around her waist as she continued walking. "How are you feeling today?"

"Mostly sore." She looked up at him. "This isn't okay. I'm supposed to be taking care of you."

His smile was a thousand watts, and her pulse jumped. "You know that frustration from not feeling useful?"

"Yes?" What was he getting at?

"Well, you are taking care of me, because I don't feel all that useless at the moment." He grinned as he helped her sit on the couch.

She rolled her eyes. "You seem to always have a way around things."

He shrugged. "I can't help that there are loopholes."

"You're such a..."

One eyebrow went up. "What?"

She wanted to say something smart, but she couldn't. He was cute and sweet. No one had taken care of her since her dad died. From the moment he took his last breath, she'd been on her own and fighting just to get from one day to the next. There was no way to thank Liam for giving her a moment to be still and have a second of peace. She wrapped her arms around his neck and hugged him. "I don't know how to say thank you so that it means as much as I want it to."

His arms enveloped her and squeezed her tightly, pulling her into his lap. "This'll work."

Why did she feel so good when she was in his arms? Anytime he was around, she wanted to be near him. His smile was like bathing in the sun. She felt safe with him. He was wonderful, but she knew it couldn't last. Not with her mom in the picture. As long as she was free, she'd make his life miserable. It was just what she did.

Goosey was gone, she'd nearly lost her life, she'd been strangled twice, her body ached, and her heart hurt. It was like an avalanche of emotions hitting her all at once. Tears welled in her eyes, and as hard as she tried to swallow everything down, she couldn't this time.

One little sob escaped, and then there was nothing she could do to hold back the tide. She balled her fists in Liam's shirt and pressed her forehead against his chest. It wasn't long after she'd started living with her mom that she learned her tears or her hurts didn't garner any kind of compassion or sympathy.

It felt like the twenty years' worth of grief was rolling through her, and her body shook with the release.

Liam tightened his arms around her. "Oh, hey, it's okay." He kissed the top of her head and gently rubbed her back. "Everything's going to be okay."

No, it wasn't. This Cinderella-esque dream was going to come to an end, and now she knew what it felt like to be held and cared for. She'd go back to the real world, and all this would be gone.

"Sara, it's going to be okay."

She didn't have words. What would she say, even if she did? That she'd fallen in love with him? The thought startled her. She loved him? As happy as the thought made her, the next thought crushed her. At the end of the week, she was going back to her life, because if she didn't, her mom would make him regret meeting her.

The sobs came harder, and breathing was nearly impossible. Her heart was thundering in her chest, and her stomach was tossing and turning.

Liam put his lips to her ear. "Sweetheart, it's okay. Take a deep breath."

This sort of thing didn't happen to her. She was the one who held people and told them it would be okay. The reason she'd become a nurse was to be there for people when they were hurting. But how long had she been hurting and holding it in because she didn't have a choice?

"Sara, breathe."

She was trying to breathe, but there wasn't enough air. Her chest was so tight it felt like she was being pressed like a grape. Everything hurt, deep and wide. She felt like an open wound, and someone was emptying a jar of salt onto her. All she wanted to do was stop hurting for a little while. Her fingers felt numb, and the grip she had on Liam's shirt loosened.

Liam called her name. She desperately wanted to answer, but she was floating away. The numb feeling in her fingers traveled up her arms and spread through her. One deep, long breath, and all she saw was darkness.

THE LAST FEW days had finally hit Sara, and she'd come undone. The perfectly composed woman he'd met three and a half weeks ago had fallen apart. She'd wept bitter, body-wracking sobs before passing out, and it had broken his heart.

The sweet woman in his arms had no idea the impact she'd had on him. In just eighteen days, she turned his world upside down in the best way possible. He wanted to do for her what she'd done for him.

To show her he loved her. Maybe if she saw it, she'd let that invisible line fade and love him back.

Sara stirred, inhaled, and then opened her eyes. "Oh, I…" She covered her face with her hands. "I've never done anything like that before."

"I'm getting a lot of your firsts." He chuckled.

She groaned. "All the bad ones."

His eyebrows went up. "I don't know. You kissed me. I don't consider it all that bad."

A tiny smile, and her eyes sparkled. "You…"

"What?" He rolled his lips in to keep from smiling.

"Nothing."

He brushed his fingertips across her cheek. "Do you feel better?"

She nodded. "Better than I have in years, actually."

"Good. You look like you feel better. You seem lighter." His gaze roamed over her face, and he kissed her forehead.

Sara sat up and wrapped her arms around his neck. Heartbeat after heartbeat ticked by without her saying a word. When she pulled back, there was something in her eyes he couldn't read. Her fingers combed through his beard as her eyes locked with his, and then she touched her lips to his.

This kiss was different. It was sweet, sensual, and intense, all rolled together.

His skin was on fire everywhere her fingers touched. She took his bottom lip in her teeth, and his heart felt like a rocket taking off. The delicate kisses were soft and languid, an intimacy he'd never experienced with any woman. With the last kiss, she deepened it, continuing the slow, unhurried kisses with a maddening effect.

She broke the kiss and said, "Thank you."

Eyes still closed, he touched his forehead to hers. He was breathless, and it felt like he was drunk. "I don't know what I did, but if you'll tell me, I'll make sure to do it again."

A small laugh. "No particular reason."

If that was a kiss for no particular reason, he couldn't imagine one that did have a reason. He felt like he was on fire. "I'll make sure you have reason next time."

"Who says there will be a next time?"

His eyes popped open, and a little smile played on her lips. Oh, he loved her. He loved everything about her. Cupping her cheek, he said, "The gala is tomorrow night. Let's go to California today. My friend is already there, and I'd like to see him before he has to leave again."

Her jaw dropped. "Today?"

"If you're feeling up to it. I know you're sore, and if

you can't, just say so." He was secretly crossing his fingers. Maybe if she got out of Denver, she could relax and it could help heal more than just her physical injuries.

She blinked a few times like she was trying to process it. "Your friend is already in town?"

"Yeah." He was busy, though, and it was less about seeing him and more about loving her.

Her teeth caught her bottom lip, and his stomach did a few turns. Man, she had to stop doing that. "Okay. When do you want to leave?"

Inside, he was doing a touchdown dance and screaming in victory. "How fast can you pack?"

She shrugged. "Everything I own is in that suitcase I brought with me."

His eyebrows drew together. "What?"

"I couldn't leave things in my room or my mom would take them. I made it to where I could zip a suitcase and put all my belongings in my car." She sat up and smiled. "I wasn't kidding when I said money doesn't mean anything to me. My mom has chased it all her life, and it's made her miserable. I didn't want that."

Liam took her face in his hands and kissed her. "Do you have anything comfortable to wear on the plane?"

She shook her head. "All I've got are those terrible

sweats and a few sets of pajamas. Everything else is business attire." Her eyebrows knitted together. "I'm not sure about going through an airport in any of my comfortable options."

That was cute. "We won't be going through an airport. I have a private jet."

Her eyebrows went up, and her mouth dropped open. "You have a private jet?"

He chuckled. "I'm a billionaire. Of course I do."

She tilted her head. "How does a football player become a billionaire, anyway?"

Most people thought of him as a big dumb jock, but he wasn't. Kimberly wouldn't let him be. "I was actually pretty good at finance in college. That's what my degree is in. I began investing when I started playing, and I got lucky on a few things. Before I knew it, there I was."

"I'm not surprised."

What? "You aren't? Everyone's surprised by that."

She gave a one-shoulder shrug and a half-smile. "I'm just not. You struck me as more than just a football player."

Liam was a little dumbfounded, but this was Sara. She saw things no one else did. "How do you do that?"

"When I was in school, all of my professors and classmates said I had a gift for reading people and situations. I don't know where it comes from." She smiled.

He held her around the waist as he stood and then set her feet on the floor. "Let me get a car up here, and we'll get to the plane. It's early enough that we could grab a late lunch in Santa Monica. Would you be okay with that?"

She tiptoed and kissed him. "I've never been there, so I'll have to trust you that it's great."

"I'll make sure it's great." He smiled. There had never been a time he was happier, especially in the last year. It felt like all the holes in his life were filling up, and the parts that had been dark were all light now. "Go get your stuff together. I'll get the arrangements made."

Her teeth caught her bottom lip as she smiled. "Okay." She didn't exactly sprint out of the room, but her pace had picked up considerably.

Liam had done something to make her happy, and it made him happy. This trip would be his love letter to her. He hoped she'd read it that way.

CHAPTER 19

*W*hen it came to arranging things, it helped when you owned a hotel on the beach. Liam stuck the card in the hotel door and opened it for Sara. Her face lit up as she gasped, and she looked around the room. The three-room suite had a full wall of windows overlooking the ocean. Of the places he loved, this was one of his favorites because of the view.

"Oh, Liam, how did you manage this on such short notice? I've never been anywhere so nice. The view is…" When she looked at him, she had tears in her eyes.

Yeah, it was fantastic, but her reaction was the best he could have hoped for. "It's my favorite."

"You've stayed here before?"

"Several times."

Her face fell.

That's not what he meant. He'd never shared this suit with another woman. This place was special, worthy of her. "No, not like that. You're the only person I've brought here."

She narrowed her eyes. "Why me?"

He locked eyes with her. "Because I knew you'd appreciate it."

Her lips curved up. "Good answer."

"Do you like it?" He was pretty sure he knew the answer, but he wanted to hear it from her.

She dropped her suitcase, walked to him, and hugged him. "I'll never be able to say thank you enough. This is the most incredible thing anyone has ever done for me."

He wrapped his arms around her, and she melted into him. "I'm glad you like it."

She pulled back. "I can't believe you managed to find something like this on such short notice."

He smiled and shrugged. "I own it."

"The suite?"

"The hotel."

She looked dumbfounded. "You own the hotel?"

Liam chuckled. "One of those lucky investments."

"I'd say so." She circled her arms around his neck again. "Thank you for inviting me."

"I wouldn't want to be here with anyone else."

"I'm going to go put my luggage up and try to find something other than pajamas to wear." She let go of him and wrapped her fingers around the suitcase handle. "Which room is mine?"

He smiled. This would be surprise number two. "I thought you might like that one." He pointed to the left.

"Okay." She walked to the room and opened the door. "This room has a view of the ocean, and there are clothes in here."

Surprise number three. He stopped behind her and smiled. "I thought you'd want to wear something comfortable other than pajamas and a little less formal than business. Since we were planning on lunch when we got here…"

She turned and hugged him again. "Why would you do all this for me?"

He wrapped his arms around her, and his heart did a little dance. "Let's just say I like to see you smile." He'd wanted to make her happy, and he felt like he'd succeeded.

Sara leaned back and held his gaze. "This is beyond words for me."

"Your smile was worth it." He grinned.

Her mouth opened and closed like she was searching for words. "You...I..." She drew her fingers across his cheek as she kept eye contact, and then her lips parted and brushed across his skin, leaving a trail of delicate kisses everywhere her fingers touched. Every time he thought her lips were going to find his, she'd hover just a breath away and then kiss his face.

It was so intoxicating that Liam braced his hand against the wall. It was either that or hit the floor. Just when he thought he'd go crazy, she crushed her lips to his, and it felt like she was trying to drink him in. Her fingers sank into his beard along his jaw, slid down his neck, and continue around his until they found his hair.

A little moan escaped from her, and his knees felt like jelly. He had no idea how long they stood there kissing, but when she pulled back, the absence of her was immediately felt.

Out of breath and flushed, she whispered, "I should get dressed so we can have lunch."

"I need to know what I did to deserve that." It was a kiss he wouldn't be forgetting anytime soon.

She nipped his lip and pulled away. "I like you." And then she smiled and shut the door.

He leaned his back against the wall and scrubbed

his face with his hands. His mind was mush. That was like? What did love feel like? He was suddenly incredibly eager to know.

Being loved by her would be worth forever. He silently sent up a prayer, hoping she'd come to the same conclusion about him by the time the trip was over.

"OH, this is good. I've never had anything so delicious." The restaurant he'd taken her to was along the beach, and the food she'd ordered was fantastic. The flaky white fish melted in her mouth, and the scallops were so sweet they were like candy.

Much like his favorite burger place, it wasn't fancy. She liked that about him. He didn't need opulent all the time to be happy. Liam didn't chase gold.

He smiled and sat back, sliding his arm along the back of the booth. His fingers found a lock of her hair and twisted it around it. "I'm glad you like it."

"Like it? I love it. I wish I could box the whole place up and take it back to Denver." She chuckled and leaned into him.

He nodded and laughed with her. "There is a temptation to do that."

She'd never been treated so well in her life. First, a hotel room with a view so beautiful it brought her to tears, then her own room with the same view so she could wake up to it, and clothes that didn't hurt. He'd gone above and beyond anything she could have ever imagined.

There had been no words, so she'd kissed him, hoping that'd say what she couldn't. That she loved him. She loved him? The thought sent little shivers down her spine. She looked at him and smiled. He was all her dreams wrapped in the most gorgeous package she could've ever imagined. She loved his smile, his goofiness, the way he would put his arms around her and hold her, his laughter, and the way his smell would wrap around her like a blanket.

She loved Liam Thomas.

How did something so bone-deep happen so quickly? And she knew it was bone deep, because the thought of not being with him was like a bird losing its wings in mid-flight.

And her mom would use his love for her as leverage and destroy him. A needle touched the little balloon of joy, and pieces of exploded rubber flew everywhere. What was she going to do? How was she going to take care of him?

By letting him go.

It was like an eclipse. Bright yellow sun and then nothing but darkness. She didn't have to let her mom take him from her yet. They were in California. She couldn't touch them there. Sara could enjoy her time with him, love him, and when she got back to Denver, she'd have this moment in time to hold on to.

She looked up at him, studying his face. That freckle she loved drawing her attention.

"What are you thinking about?" Liam asked, his eyes narrowing like he was trying to read her thoughts.

She caught her bottom lip between her teeth and smiled. "That I'm glad I was more stubborn than you."

He laughed. "I have to agree."

"What do you want to do after this?" she asked, silently pledging to hear his laughter as much as she could between now and the time they got home.

Liam shook his head. "Nope. What do *you* want to do? We can walk on the pier, go to the beach, go shopping. Whatever you want to do."

Her eyebrows knitted together. "Me?" Talk about a new experience.

"You." The way his gaze held hers made her heart stutter.

She scrunched her face up. "I still need a dress for the gala tomorrow." The ones she'd picked out before didn't work. They'd fit too tightly and the fabric had irritated the road rash on her hip.

"Then we'll go dress shopping." He shrugged.

Just when she thought he couldn't surprise her anymore. "You'd go with me?"

His eyebrows went up. "To see you in a dress? I don't see where that's a chore."

Chris never wanted to do anything like that with her. Not that she blamed him, because it was shopping. "Are you sure?"

"I'm positive. Do you want to do that next? Or something else?" he asked.

Waiting until the last minute seemed like a good way to end up with no dress. "I think that should be next in case I have trouble finding one."

His arm curled around her, pulling her closer. "Okay."

She rubbed her thumb over his lips. "Thank you for all of this."

He smiled, and it was just as good as one of his hugs. "I'm the one who needed a date. I should be thanking you."

"True. You're welcome." She pulled her lips in to keep from grinning.

The light banter stopped the moment he cupped

her cheek and brought his lips down to hers. It was something out of a movie. "Thank you."

Oh yeah, this was a wholly unique experience for her.

"Let's finish eating and go find you a dress." He touched his lips to hers again. "I already know that whatever you pick, you'll be the most beautiful woman there."

She hooked her finger around the neck of his button-up. "You're very charming; you know that?"

The smile that spread on his lips made her glad she was sitting down. "Only for you."

Looking down, she shook her head. Two could play that game. When she looked back up, her bottom lip was caught between her teeth, and she smiled. For some reason that always made his cheeks light up.

He narrowed his eyes. "I might be charming, but you don't play fair."

A one-shoulder shrug. "I don't know what you're talking about."

The laugh he gave her was so deep and rich it made her insides gooey. "We're never getting out of here if we don't cut it out."

"One last thing."

His eyes narrowed. "What?"

She held his face and kissed him. Then she pressed

her cheek to his. She couldn't say what she wanted to. If she ever told him she loved him, that'd be it. There would be no way she could ever stop saying it.

"What was that for?"

Sara pulled back and grinned. "You being you."

CHAPTER 20

"You are going to get so tired of this." Sara's shoulder sagged as she looked at Liam. A six-foot-something, hulking football player could not possibly enjoy dress shopping.

He laughed. "I'm fine. Why are you so worried?"

Because by now, Chris would have said hateful things, and she'd have left in tears, feeling worthless. Not Liam. He was sitting in the third dress shop, just smiling at her. Like he was actually having a good time because he was with her. "I don't know."

"I'm fine. Stop worrying." He stood and walked to her. "As long as I'm with you, I'm good."

"Charmer." She tiptoed and kissed him. "This one isn't it. It's scratchy, and it hurts."

He pushed her hair over her shoulder, and his eyebrows drew together. "Are you okay?"

"I'm okay. All this moving around has helped, but the couple of spots on my hip and side sting when anything rough touches it." And at that moment, the dress she was in was killing her, and it didn't look good on her at all. She wanted to look…better than great. She wanted his jaw to drop. She wanted to dress for him.

Liam bent down and kissed her bare shoulder. "Then on to the next. If you can't find something comfortable, we won't go."

What? Not go? "You have to go."

"Not without you, and not if you're hurting."

"But…"

He took her face in his hands and said, "No. That award is great, but I pick you, Sara. Okay?"

Whoa. She absentmindedly nodded. He picked her. No one ever picked her. "On to the next."

With a wink, he walked back to the chair and sat down.

Sara walked back into the dressing room and slipped off the itchy, scratchy dress and waited a moment. Her side was burning from the fabric used. When the pain subsided, she pulled on the next dress. When it was in place, she smiled. It was the one. The bodice was off the shoulder and hugged her while the skirt was organza lined with satin that skimmed the floor. It was soft and flowy with an empire waist, so it didn't really touch her side and hip.

The color was a perfect green that complimented her skin tone and brought out the color of her eyes. Her hair even looked great with it. It gave her a boost of confidence. Hanging out with all those rich people made her stomach squishy. "This is the one," she called.

"Let me see it."

She smiled as she turned and admired the dress. "Nope, it's going to be a surprise."

"What?"

Holding in a laugh, she waited as she heard footfalls.

"You mean you aren't going to let me see it until tomorrow? That's mean, Sara Lynch."

She peeked her head out. "If you see it now, it'll just be a dress. If you see it tomorrow, it'll be more than that."

"More than that, huh?" He pressed his finger under her chin and kissed her. "Then I'll wait until tomorrow with bated breath."

Tingles washed over her like waves hitting a shore, cool and foamy, sinking in and making her feel incredible. It was a cruel joke. Having a taste of something this sweet and then knowing she'd never be allowed to keep it. "I'll get dressed, and we can find something less boring to do."

"Do you need shoes?"

She'd almost forgotten about that. "Yeah, but I think I can find a pair here, so it shouldn't take long."

"Take as long you need. I'm not in a hurry." He winked.

He was a high school crush. The picture in a frame that you held to your chest as you collapsed on the bed, smiling. He was that giddy feeling that made your stomach flutter with butterflies. "Okay."

Despite his willingness to endure hours of shopping, Sara was ready to see California. She quickly changed and then found a pair of simple silver heels that complimented the accents on the dress.

When she was done, he asked the store to deliver her purchases to the hotel, and they set off to explore. Or she did, since she'd never been there before.

"Where would you like to go?" he asked as they walked out of the shop.

She shrugged. "The only thing I know about Santa Monica is the pier."

He smiled. "Want to go?"

"Sure." It sounded like fun, and it would definitely be an experience she could sock away for later.

Liam twined his fingers in hers and then pressed his lips to the back of her hand. "Then it's a date."

It was all she could do to continue standing. "Okay."

They walked down the street, holding hands, and she tried to take it all in. It was beautiful. Sunny, bright, populated with throngs of people. Going from snowcapped mountains to warm breezes was quite the temperature change too.

Once they reached the pier, her lips spread into a smile she couldn't stop. It was amazing. "Do you think we could ride the carousel?"

"Absolutely." He winked.

She was so excited it took an effort to not clap like a seal. He had no idea what it meant to her. People didn't do things she wanted to do. They didn't take her into consideration when they made plans. Her mom treated her like an afterthought, and with the way they'd moved around when she was a kid, there were no such things as friends. Even if she did have a friend, it was only at school.

On the first ride, she picked a horse on the inside. Liam stood with her as she rode, never once looking put out. He wasn't exactly carousel size. The next two rides, they sat in the sleigh and cuddled. They spent hours, drifting from one thing to the next, taking their time until the sun started going down.

"Want to walk on the beach?" he asked as they stepped off the pier.

Sara nodded. "I'd love to." Watching the sunset with him. What could be a more perfect way to end the day?

LIAM LOVED WATCHING SARA. With each new experience, it was like the weight she carried became lighter. Her smile was the best, the way her eyes sparkled when she looked at him when she was excited. Seeing her happy made him happy.

"Thank you for today. It was incredible, and a double thank you for riding the carousel with me." She squeezed his hand.

It had been as much fun for him as it was her. "I enjoyed it."

Her eyebrows went up. "Really?"

"Why would you think I wasn't having fun?" He was curious to hear her answer. Being with her, wherever it was, was fun.

A one-shoulder shrug, and she looked down as

they walked. "I don't know. If it wasn't what Chris wanted to do, he hated it. He'd complain and mope until I couldn't take it anymore, and then we'd go do what he wanted to do. After a while, I stopped caring."

"He's an idiot." But Liam was grateful he'd been one. If he was stupid enough to let Sara go, he didn't deserve her.

She chuckled. "After he won his money, all the little red flags became huge ones. He was controlling and mean. I don't know why he got it in his head, but he thought I was after his money when I never asked for anything. He'd take me to dinner, and I'd pay for my own meal. He was completely paranoid."

"Why did you break up?" He was especially curious about that.

Sara stopped. "Mind if we sit?"

"No." He stopped, and they sat together close enough to the water's edge that they could see it roll onto shore. "Going to answer my question?"

She tucked a piece of hair behind her ear as she nodded. "We'd only been dating about six months when he won. From that point forward, I have no idea why I stayed. Maybe it was just comfortable. Or maybe he was just someone and I didn't want to be alone."

"Okay." He made sure it sounded like she needed to continue.

"We never lived together, but he'd given me a key. Sometimes, when I got off work early, I'd fix dinner for us at his place." She paused. "One night, he broke the door down to my apartment because money had gone missing and he thought I'd taken it. What would have made him think that, I have no idea."

Liam didn't like where this story was going one bit. "And?"

She drew her knees up to her chest and hugged them. "He wanted to know what I'd done with his money. He tore through my place like it was an FBI search. Shredded my furniture, everything. When he didn't find it, he thought he could beat it out of me. He didn't get very far because my next-door neighbor had called the cops the moment she heard the door break."

His blood was boiling, he was so angry. "If I ever see him again, he's going to leave hurting. Did you press charges?"

"Of course I did. I wanted any woman he dated next to have a warning, but he had money and hired a good lawyer. I filed a restraining order on him, and he walked away without so much as a blemish on his record."

He gritted his teeth. "Well, he broke that order, and

if they catch him, I'll show him the meaning of a good lawyer. There won't be any walking away this time."

"My mom talked him into it. I doubt he's even still in Denver. If he is and he gets caught," she said and laughed, "I'll be perfectly fine with that."

Liam put his arm around her and pulled her to him. "Good. Most women wave it off. They shouldn't. If someone touches you in any way you don't like, tell the police. If nothing else, it gives them something for later if the jerk does it again."

She chuckled. "Having a sister puts it all in perspective."

"And if anyone touches her, they'll find out just how good I am at football." They would too. The first time he met William, he made sure to let him know that if laid a hand on her, he'd lose it.

Sara bumped him with her shoulder. "You know, your bark is a lot worse than your bite. I can't see you putting your hands on anyone."

"I haven't, ever. Other than the football field. I've never had a reason to so far. If I warn someone, it's usually good enough to keep them straight." He smiled.

She snorted. "Well, yeah, you're as big as a house."

"And it works in my favor."

They sat quietly a second, and then he pulled her

over his lap and hugged her to him. "Thank you for coming with me."

Her arms circled his neck. "This has been the most incredible experience. Thank you for inviting me."

"I'm glad you've had fun. I know I have. I needed out of Denver for a minute. Out of that house." His arm grazed her leg, and his jaw dropped. "You're freezing."

She nuzzled his neck with her nose. "I'm fine."

"What's your definition of fine?" he asked, chuckling.

A long sigh ,and she said, "With you."

That wasn't the answer he was expecting, but he'd take it. He curled himself around her and tightened his hold. "Our definitions line up."

Covering her mouth with her hand, she yawned. "I'm so sorry."

"Tired?" He suspected she was. It'd been a long day for someone who'd nearly been dragged off a mountain.

She laid her head on his shoulder and nodded. "Yeah, but I've had so much fun today that it was worth it." Her fingers ran along his jaw and into his beard. She sat up and touched her lips to his.

What was it about her that made everything fall away? He slipped his hand into her hair and held her as she kissed him. If there was such a thing as the exclamation point to the end of a day, this was it. He deepened the kiss, and she molded against him. No one had ever fit like her. She filled all his empty spaces.

Sea salt and her light fruity shampoo swirled around him. Every time she kissed him, he didn't think it could get any better, and each time it was. He pulled back as she nipped his bottom lip. "I think I could live on your kisses."

"Well, then I guess they'll all have to belong to you." She plunged her fingers into his hair and crushed her lips to his.

Oh yeah, he'd take that deal every day, all day long. If all her kisses belonged to him, he wondered if he could have the rest of her too. He sure wanted her.

For hours, she kissed him like each one was the last she'd ever give him. Each one headier than the last. By the time they broke apart and returned to the hotel room, it was well into the night.

She kissed him one more time and then slipped behind her door. He didn't know what she was going to do, but he was headed for the shower, a long icy one. Sleeping was going to be impossible.

CHAPTER 21

*A*big, bright yellow sun hung high in the sky as Sara awoke. The make-out session on the beach came roaring to the front of her mind. It'd taken forever to get to sleep the night before. The feel of his lips on hers. If she closed her eyes, she was still there on the beach, encased in his arms.

She sat up, and her body complained about the amount of activity from the day before. It was the most she'd done since she'd been released from the hospital, but she wasn't about to say anything. It was so much fun spending the day with Liam. The pier was amazing. He'd ridden the carousel with her three times.

Yesterday would be a day she'd never forget, and it was all because of him. Everything was better when she was with him because she loved him. The line had been crossed, and she wasn't sure how she was going to redraw it when they returned to Denver.

She pushed the covers off and stood, anxious to see him. When she opened the door, his smile greeted her, and her pulse jumped. "Hi."

He stood and walked to her. "Hey, you feeling okay?"

"I'm okay. What time is it?" she asked.

His arm wrapped around her waist, and he kissed her forehead. "It's a little after one."

She leaned into him. "After one? How long have you been up?"

"A few hours, but I figured you'd pushed yourself yesterday and you needed the sleep." He tucked a piece of her hair behind her ear. "Are you hungry?"

Her stomach growled. "Um, I guess I am."

"Breakfast or lunch?"

She didn't care as long as it was food. "I'm okay with whatever."

He narrowed his eyes. "Stay in or go out?"

Her body pointed its finger at her and gave her a dirty look. "In?"

"You got it." He smiled and kissed her nose.

While he ordered room service, she took a shower. It helped loosen her stiff muscles, and she could walk a little easier. The next time she came out, she felt considerably better, and the suite was filled with mouthwatering aromas.

"The shower helped?" he asked.

She nodded. "A lot. Something smells great. What all did you get?"

He shrugged. "I figured a little bit of breakfast and lunch so you could pick through what you wanted or what sounded good."

"Thank you." There was more food than she'd ever be able to eat, but all of it looked good. She picked out a few things and sat on the couch. "This is great."

"What would you like to do today?" he asked as he finished filling his plate and sat beside her.

Good question. She had no idea. "I don't know. It's already after one, and you have your award presentation tonight. Do we have time to do anything?"

"It's not until seven. Even leaving a few hours to get ready, we have some time to kill." He took a few bites of bacon and chased it with some water.

She didn't care what they did as long as she was with him. "I really don't know what to do."

He sat forward and put his plate on the coffee table. "You were pretty sore when you first came out. Maybe it wouldn't be a bad idea to stay in."

She chewed her thumb. "Good point. A lazy day inside doesn't sound all that bad."

"I can go for lazy." He grinned and took a bite of the cheeseburger he'd ordered.

They finished eating, and Liam covered his mouth with his hand as he yawned. "I guess I should have slept longer."

"It is a lazy day." She smiled. "You could take a nap. I even have a lap you could use."

He chuckled. "That sounds good."

She pulled the ottoman closer and propped her feet up, crossing them at the ankle, and then patted her leg. "I'm ready."

Liam stretched and then twisted around to face her as he laid his head on her lap. She slowly combed her fingers through his hair and studied his face. It was covered in freckles, not heavily, but covered. Even his eyelids had them. If she could, she'd kiss each one individually.

"Why are you looking at me like that?" he asked.

Because if she could, she'd smother him in kisses, tell him how much she loved him, and ask to stay with him forever. "I like your freckles."

He pressed his cheek against her stomach and closed his eyes as he chuckled. "I don't think anyone's ever said that before."

Then they're nuts, she thought. She ran her fingertips from one temple to the other, following the freckles like a dot-to-dot puzzle. He took a deep breath and groaned.

A smile crept on his face. "Keep doing that, and I won't be awake long."

She continued the light touches, and he inhaled deeply a few more times. Then his body relaxed, and his breathing was even. If this is what a lazy day with him looked like, she'd be first in line to sign up.

Things had changed so much between them in such a short time. If anyone had told her she'd fall head over heels for someone in less than three weeks, she'd have laughed in their face. It wasn't possible—until it was.

She caressed his cheek with the back of her hand and then straightened her fingers and threaded them through his hair. He moaned in his sleep, and she smiled. Even in his sleep, it seemed he enjoyed her company.

It felt good to be wanted, and he'd made her feel wanted, especially the day before. She was going to enjoy her remaining time with him. Soak him up, burn his smile into her memory, and hold on with two fists to the feeling of being cared for.

She bent down and pressed her lips to his. There'd

never be another man she'd love as much as she loved him.

BUTTONING HIS CUFFLINKS, Liam took one last look in the mirror. He'd never been more excited to take a woman out in his life. And he'd never been more interested in a dress before. She'd be beautiful no matter what, but his curiosity was at an all-time high.

He pulled the black suit coat on, buttoned the middle button, and walked out of his room. Waiting for her was torture. Not that he minded waiting for her, he just didn't like being away from her.

Pulling out his phone, he glanced at her door and hit the call button. He'd had Goosey pulled up and wanted to know the verdict. A friend of his owned a body shop in El Paso, and he'd had it trailered and taken down there. "It's Liam. What's it looking like, Mike?"

"It's bad. Man, I'm good, but I'm not a fairy godmother. This thing is crunched. I might be able to find a rolling body and then salvage some pieces from it. That's as good as I can get it."

It wasn't what he wanted to hear, but he'd been expecting it. Mike had sent him pictures, and it was barely recognizable as a car. If Sara saw it, it'd break her heart all over again.

"Do whatever you have to do. I want it to look brand new when she sees it again." Hopefully, it would be close enough that she'd be a little pieced back together.

"I'll give it my best shot."

Liam exhaled. "Thanks, Mike." He ended the call just as Sara's door opened, and his heart skipped a beat. She was breathtaking. It was a simple green empire-waisted dress with a skirt almost touching the floor. Her hair was pulled to the side and pinned up.

She chewed her bottom lip as she walked out and stopped. "Do you like it?"

Like it? More like loved it. He crossed the room. "It's like it was handpicked for you. You look incredible."

"I'm sorry I took so long. I tried to cover the scratches on my face, but the makeup made them look worse, so I washed it off." She touched her cheek with her fingertips.

He tipped her chin up with a single finger. "You look beautiful. Absolutely beautiful."

"You look like a model." She ran her fingers through his beard, tiptoed, and kissed him. "I love your beard."

If she loved it, it would stay. "Most women don't like it."

"No accounting for taste." She shrugged and smiled.

"I have something for you to go with your dress." He winked and grabbed a flat velvet box from the coffee table.

Her eyes went wide. "I don't need anything else, Liam. What you've done for me already is enough."

Liam shook his head. "I'm not doing this for you. I'm doing it for me." He handed her the box, and she held his gaze for a moment.

When she opened the box, her lips parted with a gasp. "Oh, this is too much. I can't wear this."

He'd picked it out earlier in the day, along with something else. "It's yours, so yes, you can."

Her mouth opened and closed a few times like she was trying to find words. "What? But I can't."

"It's just a simple platinum and diamond necklace, Sara. It's nothing big. I knew you'd like it because it's delicate, like you."

She lifted an eyebrow, and he knew she was about to say something smart. "You do know the words simple and diamond don't really go together, right? Especially when you throw the word platinum in there."

"I want you to have it."

Her teeth caught her bottom lip, and she stared at it. "It's so pretty."

"Turn around, and I'll put it on, if you'd like."

Her lips spread into a wide smile, and she turned. "I can't believe you bought this for me. Why?"

Liam pulled the necklace out of the box, fastened it around her neck, and then bent down and pressed his lips against her cheek. He wanted to say, "Because I love you," but what came out of his mouth was, "Because I wanted to."

She touched the necklace and blinked as she faced him. "Why me?"

Why? The reasons were limitless. "You're witty, kind, and caring. And because I like to make you smile."

Sara cupped his cheek. "I don't need things from you to make me smile. A kiss would have gotten you the same reaction."

"Mind if I test that theory?" He'd wanted to kiss her, and with an in like that, he wasn't about to miss it.

She shook her head. "Not like I have makeup to ruin." She pointed a finger at him. "Just don't mess up my hair. That took forever."

He chuckled and bent down, touching his lips to hers and gathering her in his arms. It was like a Fourth of July fireworks display. She circled one arm around his neck and held his face with her hand. He deepened the kiss and reveled in the taste of her. He knew they had to be somewhere, and he didn't care.

Sara broke the kiss and pressed her forehead to his. "You have an award to accept. It's kinda why I got the dress."

"I'd rather kiss you," he said and kissed her throat.

"And your friend is there."

"I have no desire to kiss him."

A tiny laugh. "We need to go."

Liam exhaled the frustration and held his arm out. "Are you ready?"

She hooked hers in his and nodded.

They walked through the hotel, and Sara never even noticed the looks she got. How could a woman so beautiful not see what everyone else saw? That necklace was nothing in comparison to her. She was the treasure, and he was going to do his best to hold on to her.

CHAPTER 22

*L*iam stepped out of the limousine, turned, and held his hand out to Sara. With a smile, she put her hand in his, and her eyes sparkled as she followed him out. She belonged at events like this more than she knew.

She hooked her arm in his as they walked down the red carpet. One of the photographers waved and said, "Just a shot of you, Liam."

Before she could move, he put his arm around her and shook his head. "You don't get me without her."

She stood on her tiptoes and whispered in his ear, "Liam, I'm not the celebrity. They don't want my picture."

"We're a package deal." He bent down and kissed

her. Camera flashes went off in rapid fire. Suddenly, the energy shifted and so did the questions.

"Who's the girl?"

"What's her name?"

"Where'd you meet?"

He smiled and shook his head. "Sorry, that's private."

Sara touched his shoulder. "There's a little girl over there. I think she wants your autograph."

Well, she did have his jersey number on. He held Sara's hand as he approached her. The little girl's face lit up.

"Would you like an autograph?"

Her head bobbed up and down.

Sara leaned in. "If you let me use your phone, I bet he'll take a picture with you."

He absolutely would.

When they were finished, the little girl turned to who he suspected were her parents and squealed.

"Boy, she loves you," Sara said.

He shrugged. "I don't know why. I'm just a football player. Ex-football player now."

The corners of her lips quirked up. "You have no clue as to why, huh?"

"No."

She lifted up and kissed him. "One of your more endearing qualities."

They finished the press obstacle course and went inside. Liam smiled as his friend, Dr. Sebastian Gambara, came into view. "Hey, Bash, long time no see." They shook hands.

"Dr. Gambara?" Sara asked.

His friend's jaw dropped. "Sara Lynch?" He took her face and kissed each cheek. "You're as beautiful today as you were six years ago."

Liam looked from Bash to Sara. "You two know each other?"

Bash chuckled. "It was my second year with Doctors Without Borders. This cute-as-a-button woman stepped off the truck, and the entire camp stopped and stared."

Sara's cheeks lit up like they were on fire. "Don't listen to him. They did not."

"I think I'll go with his version. I suspect it's more accurate." Liam grinned. He loved it when she blushed.

Bash kept his eyes on Sara. "She was the most gifted nurse. I'd never had anyone look at someone and just know what was going on."

Boy, did Liam know that. She had him figured out in seconds. "I've got firsthand knowledge of that."

His friend's smile faded. "Biggest mistake I ever made was letting her leave."

She smiled as she looked up at him. "Don't listen to him. We were good friends. He's a great doctor. One of the best I've ever worked with."

Bash nodded, but if Liam was reading it right, his friend had wanted more. "We *were* good friends." There was a wistfulness to his voice...a missed opportunity.

Sara tiptoed and kissed Liam on the cheek. "I'm going to run to the lady's room. I'll be right back."

The moment she was out of earshot, Liam turned on Bash. "You had feelings for her."

"And she was clueless. I tried to tell her, but she'd wave me off. She's the one that got away." Bash turned his attention to Liam.

Liam looked over his shoulder in Sara's direction, and his mouth dropped open. *"That's Sara?"* He could still remember the conversation he'd had with Bash after she'd left. His heart had been broken.

His friend nodded. "That's Sara. If you hurt her, Liam, I'll find you and cut you into so many tiny pieces they'll never be able to identify the body."

He would do his best to never hurt her again. "I'm in love with her."

"Yeah, she's pretty easy to love. Has no idea her value or how special she is. I was stupid; don't be like me." The loss was evident in his voice.

Liam grasped his shoulder. "I'm sorry, Bash. I had no idea."

"She's in love with you too. You can see it in the way she looks at you. My time has come and gone."

Sara returned and slipped her arm around Liam's. "So, did I miss anything good?"

"Just guy talk," Bash said.

"I can't believe you're here, Bash. It's so good to see you." She captured her bottom lip between her teeth and smiled.

He lifted an eyebrow. "Still killing them with that, huh?"

"What?"

Liam snorted. He knew exactly what Bash was talking about. That little nibble of her lip was like kryptonite.

"Nothing." He laughed and caught Liam's eyes. "Nothing at all."

Sara narrowed her eyes. "I'm missing something."

Bash tipped his head toward the tables. "Let's go sit down."

It wasn't long after they sat down that their meals were delivered. For event food, it was great. Much better than any she'd ever had. Guess that's what rich-people event food was like. No tough chicken or cold steak for them.

Sara felt her phone vibrate through her purse and peeked at the caller id. Her mom? After what happened in the hospital?

The call stopped, and a text message came next.

Sara, please call me. Please. I need to talk to you.

Sara looked up from her phone and managed to hold the smile on her face as Liam's fingers brushed across her shoulder. Even as distracted as she was, her skin still tingled at his touch. She should ignore Regina.

Her phone vibrated again, and she glanced down.

Please, Sara. Just one call. After that, I'll never bother you again.

Her mom had never said that before. Could one call hurt? All she had to do was hang up if she didn't like where it was going.

She leaned into Liam. "I need to run to the restroom, okay?"

"Sure, sweetheart. I'll be waiting right here for you."

Why did that pet name make her shiver? Because it

was coming from him. "I won't be long." She pressed her lips to his, stood, and walked to the bathroom. The second she found an empty stall, she dialed her mom.

"Sara?"

"What do you want, Regina?"

"It's so loud."

Next thing she'd want would be to know where Sara was, but she wasn't telling her that. She didn't feel bad lying to her if it protected Liam. "I'm at a concert in Colorado Springs. What do you want?"

"I want to tell you how sorry I am." It almost sounded like her mom's voice held a tinge of sadness. And she didn't try to pry out her whereabouts? What was going on?

Sara scoffed. "Right. I'm sure you're just wrecked at the way you've treated me."

"I am. Getting hauled out of that hospital by two cops was the worst. At first, I was really angry, but the more I thought about it, the more ashamed I became. It was a wake-up call. I've been horrible to you. I took you because you came with money when I should have wanted you because you were mine."

Sara's heart nearly stopped. She couldn't be hearing what she was hearing. Her mom apologizing? Sounding genuinely sincere? What?

Her mom continued. "I know you have no reason

to trust me. If I were in your shoes, I'd cut all ties and be done with me."

"The first good idea you've had."

"I deserve that. I deserve all your anger and your hate for what I've done to you."

Sara was speechless. Who was this woman that sounded like her mom?

"I am so sorry. I know you don't owe me anything, but if there is even an ounce of try left in you, would you let me try to make it up to you? Could we work on building a relationship like we're supposed to have?" Her mom's voice broke. "I know it'll take years to gain your trust, but I'll do anything and everything in my power to get it back. If you just give me the chance."

It was like her mom had reached inside one of her dreams and pulled out everything Sara had ever wanted to hear. "I don't know."

"I understand. If you'd like, we can meet at a restaurant in a few days. There's no pressure, and I'll understand if you decide not to show up."

Sara blinked. The conversation was so surreal she took the phone from her ear and checked the caller id again. It read: Regina. It even had the correct phone number. It had to be her, but it didn't sound like her. "I'll think about it."

"I'll text you the restaurant and let you know what time, but like I said, there's no pressure."

"Okay."

"Sara, I love you, and I'm sorry it's taken me so long to wake up."

They said their goodbyes, and Sara ended the call. Sara covered her mouth with her hand. How was she keeping it together?

It was everything Sara had ever wanted to hear. Her mom, apologetic, tearfully asking for forgiveness and a chance to rebuild their relationship, knowing that it would take time for them to get where it should be.

Sara didn't know what she wanted to do other than she wanted to be loved by her mom. She'd been desperate for her mom's affection since she was eight. If there was even a slight chance she could have a relationship with her, she'd take it.

Sara squared her shoulders and walked back the table. This was Liam's night, and she wouldn't let anything detract from that. She smiled as she sat next to him.

Liam leaned over and put his lips next to her ear. "My turn. I'll be right back, okay?"

"Okay," she said and kissed him as he stood.

"He cares about you, you know," Bash said as Liam walked away.

She nodded. Yeah, he did care about her. "He's incredibly sweet. I enjoy spending time with him."

"You know it's more than that, right?" he asked and held her gaze.

She waved him off. Liam was sweet, and they'd had a great time together. That didn't mean this trip could spill over to the rest of her life. Yeah, they'd kissed, but this was a getaway. It wasn't serious. She loved Liam, and she wanted him to love her, but that didn't mean he did. Thinking it could be more would only make it harder when it came time to leave. Until she was sure Regina couldn't hurt him, she wouldn't even explore the possibility. The direction of the conversation needed to change. "How have you been?"

A thin smile spread on his lips like he knew what she was doing. "I've been okay. You haven't changed a bit."

"Oh, stop." She shook her head. He was always so sweet.

Bash tilted his head. "You haven't. Still just as unaware of your beauty now as you were then."

Her cheeks were burning. "Bash, stop."

"Can I ask what happened?" He slid his finger across his cheek and down his jaw.

She touched her cheek. "It's kind of a long story. The brakes on my car gave out, and my shirt got caught on the door of my car. It almost pulled me over a mountain."

His eyes widened. "What?"

"It was kind of a freak thing. Liam's home is on the side of a mountain, and I was trying to get a book out. It was actually terrifying." Now she could chuckle; right after, it would have led to her having a breakdown.

Liam returned, kissing her cheek as he sat next to her. "Hey."

"So, how did the two of you meet?" Sara asked.

Bash laughed. "He came into the emergency room in Denver. It was my last year of residency. In fact, I was a week away from being done. This guy comes in with a broken arm."

Sara looked at Liam. "What did you do?"

"Yeah, Liam, what were you doing?" Bash smiled like it was a best-kept secret.

Liam's entire face turned as red as his hair. "I had some friends who were BMX bike racers. I thought it wasn't that hard, and it turned out I was wrong. I tried to pull a trick stunt, landed wrong, and broke my arm."

She was having trouble imagining him on a bike,

much less trying to do a racing trick. "I'm having trouble picturing it."

"I shouldn't have talked smack, but I was a lot younger and incredibly immature." Liam laughed.

Before the conversation could continue, a woman took the stage and began speaking. She thanked everyone for coming and gushed about the people who were receiving recognition for their generosity.

Liam was right. Why would you even want an award for doing something good? He wouldn't have even come to it if it weren't for Bash. It gave her a tinge of pride to know Liam didn't care about getting an award.

Once the last award was given, the rest of the night was a blur between dancing and talking to Bash. It was a little stuffy while the awards were given out, but overall, it was pretty fun. Not once did anyone make her feel out of place. She was especially glad Katarina hadn't shown. If Sara never saw her again, it'd be fine with her.

The conversation with her mom was never far from her mind. During the presentation, she'd decided to meet her mom. What if her mom *was* being sincere? All these years, Sara had wanted a relationship with her mom that wasn't toxic. If Regina was ready for that, Sara wanted to at least give it a try, especially if it meant she could be with Liam without fear that her mom would target him.

More than anything, Sara loved Liam; if she could be with him, it was worth the risk.

CHAPTER 23

Standing in front of the wall of windows, Sara looked out over the horizon. She couldn't imagine getting used to the view. It was something she would have never experienced had she not been with Liam. And she wouldn't have wanted to without him. He was part of what made everything so great.

His door opened, and she glanced over her shoulder. "Hey." He made her pulse jump every time she saw him. Tuxedo, jeans and t-shirt, or anything else, it didn't matter; he looked good to her.

He walked to her, put his arms around her, and kissed her neck. "Hi."

"Look at that view." No matter how much she tried, she couldn't take it all in. "It's simply beautiful."

"Yeah, it is." He held her face and kissed her. "You ready to grab some breakfast? I thought since the plane didn't leave until this afternoon, we could walk along the beach one more time before we left."

She smiled. "I'd love that." If she could, she would have added, "And I love you."

It made the hope that her mom was being genuine run a little deeper. If her mom was done being a con artist, if she would leave Liam and his friends and family alone, Sara would tell him she loved him.

There *was* the chance he didn't love her. A trip was great, and it did mean something, but it didn't necessarily translate to love. She wanted it, too, because if this was his kind of love, she wanted to bask in it. It was sweet and tender.

"Then let's go." He kissed her cheek and took her hand.

They left the hotel, found a small breakfast place a few blocks away, and sat close together as they ate. Once they were finished, they went for a walk on the beach and stayed there until it was time to fly out.

With each mile, Denver got closer, and the deepest sadness she'd ever felt settled over her. If her mom was faking it, this would be the last time she'd see Liam. That morning, she'd rented a car, and it would be waiting when they landed.

She took a deep breath and let it out. There was a little time left, and she'd spend her little bit of time happy.

An hour into the flight, Sara looked out over the horizon as the plane flew past puffy white clouds. Rolling her head, she looked at Liam. "This was the most fun I've ever had." And she knew why, but she wouldn't say anything. Not until she'd spoken to her mom.

"I had a great time too. Thanks for coming with me. We should do it again." He grinned.

She chuckled. "Oh, right, just drop everything and take a jaunt to California."

"Or Paris, Amalfi coast, Hawaii, or anywhere else we wanted."

Her brain hiccupped. She couldn't imagine going any of those places, but by the look on Liam's face, he was dead serious. "You're being completely serious, aren't you?"

"Yeah. I think traveling with you would be fun. I like how you see things. You get excited over stuff other people overlook." He pulled her over his lap. "And most of all, I enjoy spending time with you."

He had no idea how much she enjoyed being with him. It didn't have to be anywhere special or exotic; as long as they were together, it was perfect. He made her feel special and wanted. How could she do the same for him? He had money, fame, and all the things that came with it.

The only time she was good with words was when she was reading a situation. Any other time, it felt like what she said was always inadequate; instead of responding, she ran her fingers through his beard and smiled as his eyes closed. Then she gently touched her lips to his until he moaned and sank his hands into her hair, holding her still as he deepened the kiss.

She circled her arms around his neck and melted into him. There were no words that would have told him what she was feeling. Kissing him was barely coming close to describing what he meant to her. If she kissed him twenty-four hours straight, it might give him a glimpse of how much she loved him.

He held her and kissed her the rest of the flight home. As the plane landed, she broke the kiss. She held his face and pressed her forehead to his. "You are special to me, Liam. No one means as much to me as you do."

Before he could speak, she kissed him again. He was going to say something that would test her willpower, and she couldn't let him do it. She loved him, and she was about to hurt him.

Liam spent the entire plane ride to Denver trying to find a way to tell Sara he loved her, but something was off. He couldn't put his finger on it, but the way she kissed him was like she was trying to say goodbye.

He thought this trip would change things for her. That it would show her they could work and crossing the line had been okay. Instead, it seemed like it'd changed nothing.

Now they'd landed, and he felt like something awful was waiting for him. Stepping off of the plane, he spotted a small car and wondered who could be at the landing strip since no one knew they were even there.

Sara stopped at the car waiting for them and looked up at him. "Kimberly knows you aren't pretending anymore, doesn't she?"

He hadn't expected that, but he should have. "How long have you known?"

"You would've never left your wheelchair behind if you hadn't told her. You love and respect her and would've never let her find out through second-hand means." She smiled. "You're better than that."

Liam looked down. Was that why she'd pulled away? "I wasn't trying to lie to you."

"And you told her to extend her honeymoon and ask me to stay an additional week."

He jerked his head up and stared. "How do you do that?"

She chuckled. "I believe Bash called me gifted."

His mouth dropped open, and he shook his head. "How long have you known that?"

"The moment you said you were leaving the wheelchair." She hugged him around the waist. "I will never forget this trip or you."

The way she said it made his pulse jump. "What's that mean?"

"I need to put my luggage in the car." Sara turned and walked toward the small car with him following.

"Sara, what are you doing?" He was already shattering.

She stopped and turned. His heart dropped. He'd seen that look before.

"Don't, Sara." He tried to keep his voice from breaking and failed.

She smiled. It was Robot Sara. "Mr. Thomas, working for you has been the best experience I've ever had. You are a good man, and given the opportunity, I would be happy to be your nurse again."

He took her by the arms. "Why are you doing this?"

"Because I have to." She pulled away and walked the rest of the way to the car.

Liam was as brain-locked as he'd ever been. He'd been ready to tell her he loved her. With a shake of his head, he strode to the car and stopped in front of her. "Would you ever be able to love me?"

"I can't cross that line, so the answer is no." She slipped into the driver's seat, and he stood there as she drove away.

He'd never felt so broken in his life. Even his hip injury hadn't hurt this bad. In three weeks, Sara had made him as happy as he had ever been and then crushed him. An ache settled into the deepest part of his heart. His chest hurt, and breathing was painful.

Why had he let himself fall in love with her? What had he thought would happen? She'd told him from the beginning that he was her client. There was a small part of him that wanted to call her back and remind her of her promise to take care of him, but he wanted all of her. Settling for anything less wouldn't be worth the pain of having her come back.

Liam walked to his car and got in. It'd be awhile before he was ready for the world again.

CHAPTER 24

"*L*iam," Kimberly called as she walked through the front door. "Liam, where are you? I've been calling you for two days."

"I don't want to talk, Kim. I'll call you when I do." He'd deliberately not answered the phone. He didn't want to talk to anyone. What he wanted was to sit in his room, in the dark, and be left alone.

She stopped at his door and crossed her arms over her chest. "Don't you start your nonsense with me. You talk right now."

He shook his head. "What's there to say? She doesn't feel the same way. I was a client. That was it."

"Start from the beginning and don't leave anything out," Kim said as she took a seat in the chair next to him.

What was the point? It'd just be rehashing what he'd already been thinking about nonstop.

Kimberly touched his arm. "Come on, little brother, spill."

Liam did as she asked and started from the beginning and finished with their conversation at the landing strip.

"So, her mom is a scam artist, and she was afraid of her getting to you?"

He nodded. "I told her I'd take care of it."

Kim lifted an eyebrow. "And she knew you'd called me so I'd ask her to stay?"

"Yeah, I don't know how, but she did. I've never met anyone who could do that." He smiled as he thought of her.

She tapped her fingers on the arm of the chair. "She said she couldn't love you, not that she didn't, right?"

"That's verbatim what she said. That it was a line she wouldn't cross." He looked away. It hurt just as much now as it did two days ago.

Kim shook her head. "Tell me exactly what she said."

He exhaled sharply and rolled his eyes. "She said, 'I can't cross that line, so the answer is no.'"

"That's can't. Not doesn't. She absolutely loves you,

and she's protecting you from her mom."

"That's not how it sounded."

"Right, because you were upset, but if you think about what she said and think about her character, what makes more sense?"

Liam stood and raked a hand through his hair. "I don't know."

"You want my advice?" she asked as she looked up at him.

He shrugged. "Sure."

Kimberly stood. "You need to hire a private investigator and have her followed. I'll bet you money she's trying to keep her mom from you. And if her mom is as bad as you say she is, there's a really good chance Sara's in trouble."

That possibility hadn't even entered his mind. Sara being in danger? Would her mom really do something to her? "You think so?"

She shrugged. "A woman who would allow an ex-boyfriend with a restraining order to come to the hospital with her and then choke her? Yeah, I'd say there's a good probability. What would it hurt to be sure? If nothing happens, you'll have your answer."

He crossed his arms over his chest. "What if I don't like the answer?"

"At least you'd have an answer." Kim took his face

in her hands. "Find your answers."

Liam nodded. "Are you staying here while William is out of town?"

Kim lifted an eyebrow. "Do you want me to? I thought you wanted your space."

"Turns out that space is overrated."

She laughed and popped him on the arm. "Yeah, I can stay. I'll get some dinner started while you start asking some questions." Kim turned and walked out of his room.

What she said made sense. What he'd felt from Sara was that she cared about him. What if she was protecting him from her mother? If there was even the slightest chance she could be in danger, he couldn't sit by and let her get hurt.

Yeah, he needed answers, and he was going to get them.

SARA TOUCHED her forehead to the steering wheel of her rental car. When she'd driven away from Liam, she'd broken her own heart. The break in his voice and the hurt in his eyes almost made her turn around. She couldn't love him, but she did. It'd been four days, and it took effort not to curl into a ball and cry again.

The restaurant Regina had picked was on the edge of town and one she'd never been to, but it was daylight and public, so she felt relatively safe. Chris's car was nowhere around, and that was a good sign too.

With a few deep gulps of air, Sara got out of the car and went into the restaurant. Her mom was sitting in the corner in the far back, and there were a few people sitting at the bar and at least three couples eating. So far, so good.

Regina smiled as she saw her and waved. Sara lifted her hand and waved back as she weaved through the tables. When she stopped, her mom stood and hugged her. It was a real hug too. The kind that squished you and made you feel loved.

"I'm so glad you came. I was hoping so much that you would." Her smile seemed so genuine. She was even dressed differently. No thin blouse or too-tight skirt. Just jeans and a basic grey t-shirt. Her hair was even different. Not teased or full of hair product, just clean and wavy.

Sara didn't know what to think. Part of her wondered if her mom had been body snatched. "You look great. I love your hair."

Her mom ran her fingers through it. "Thanks. It feels better."

"I'm sorry for being so suspicious, but—"

"I deserve it. I've treated you so horribly since you were little, thinking of you as nothing more than an ATM. I'm so sorry. Being forcibly removed from a hospital by security was so embarrassing. It was a hospital, for crying out loud. What was I thinking?"

Sara had wondered the same thing.

Her mom continued. "And bringing Chris. I was such an idiot."

"What brought this all on? You've had run-ins with security before." Sara's eyebrows drew together.

Regina looked away and then looked back. "I don't know. I went straight from the hospital to a bar and was about to take a drink. This woman sat next to me and asked why I looked so upset, and I told her." She grunted. "She was the bluntest woman I've ever met. She said I needed to clean my act up. That I'd nearly lost my daughter, a daughter who'd taken care of me. We must have talked for hours. It was like a switch was flipped."

Sara felt like a shaken soda. Everything inside of her fizzed, and her breathing was ragged. This was what she'd wanted her entire life. "After all this time?"

"I will never be able to beg long enough for your forgiveness. You're beautiful, bright, and successful. I couldn't be prouder of you. I think maybe I was jealous. You had yourself so together, and I was such a mess. I still am, but I don't want to be anymore." Her mom stretched her hand across the table and took Sara's hand. "I am so, so sorry."

Her head was spinning. "I've wanted a relationship with you for so long. I've wanted to be loved by you. I'd really like to try."

Regina sighed. "I'm so glad to hear you say that. I want to try too. I know I'll make more mistakes because I've spent so long making them, but I will do my best to make it up to you."

A waitress came to the table and set a drink in front of Sara.

"I hope you don't mind. When the waitress took my order, I ordered you a soda." Regina lifted her glass. "I got root beer and thought you'd like the same."

Sara covered her mouth with her hand. If her mom was actually trying to change, maybe she could love Liam. She could have both of them. She picked up her drink and downed half of it. "Thank you." She'd been so nervous she'd been afraid to put anything in her stomach, and she was thirsty.

"How was your concert in Colorado Springs?" her mom asked.

She was still being cautious. "It was great. I just needed out of town a few days, so I rented a car and went."

Her mom laughed. "I was surprised that you'd go to something like that."

"I was too. It's not really something I'd normally do." She picked up her drink and finished it off. "I was thirsty. I think I should order water next."

Regina scrunched her nose. "I got a job, and I've rented an apartment."

Her mom got a job and an apartment? "What?"

"Yeah, I sold a bunch of stuff. It's a real hole-in-the-wall, but it's mine and I paid for it. If you aren't starving, would you want to go see it? Maybe after, we can get a bite to eat." She smiled.

Sara blinked a few times. The dizzy feeling returned. It was like she was in an alternate reality. "Let's go."

Her mom threw a few dollars on the table, and Sara could've cried. She hadn't asked anything of her. They stood and walked out of the restaurant. By the time they got to the car, Sara felt warm and sluggish.

"This is your car?" her mom asked.

The rental wasn't fancy, but it was nicer than Goosey. Yeah, and it got a ton better gas mileage. A subcompact would do that, as opposed to her boat of a car.

"I need a second. I think I'm overwhelmed." Sara laughed.

Regina touched her forehead. "The flu has been going around. Do you want to sit down?"

"Yeah."

As she pulled off her coat, her mom opened the car door, and she sat. She was so lightheaded, and she could barely keep her eyes open. Something tight began wrapping around her wrists, and she looked down. "What are you doing?" Then she realized she was sitting in the back seat.

Her mom's lips curled up. "I'm taking you to see your boyfriend."

"Chris? He's not my boyfriend. I broke up with him." Her head dropped onto the back of the seat.

"I was thinking more like Liam Thomas."

"What did you do?" It was a struggle to stay awake.

Her mom tapped her cheek. "A little insurance to keep you agreeable."

Sara fell sideways in the seat.

"And just like that, he's anxious to see you." Her mom held up Sara's phone and showed her the text message.

She was going to have to keep herself awake, and she was so groggy.

"You take a little nap. I'll wake you when we get there," Regina said as she slammed the back door shut and got into the driver's seat of Sara's rental.

CHAPTER 25

A smack to the cheek snapped Sara to attention, or as much as she could. Whatever her mom had given her was strong. Her mom grabbed her by the arm and pulled her out of the car.

"Come on; we need to talk to Liam."

Sara shook her head. "No. We're not together. He's just a client." The words were hard to get out.

Regina put her arm around her waist and something sharp poked her in the ribs. "We're going to walk, and you're going to do as you're told. Got it?"

"Are you going to shoot me if I don't?" It sounded like garble to her ears.

Her mom put her mouth to her ear. "No, I'm going to shoot him."

Oh no. Sara needed to do something to keep her from hurting Liam.

They walked together to the front door, and Regina knocked.

"Sara," Liam said as he opened the door with a smile. Then his face fell.

"Step back." Regina gouged the gun in her ribs again.

Liam held his hands up and took a few steps back.

Kimberly walked into the living room and stopped. "What's going on?" Then her eyes widened. "Oh."

"I knew my daughter had something going on with someone. Imagine my surprise when I see a photograph of her on a gossip site with Liam Thomas." She stuck the gun in Sara's ribs again as she used her foot to shut the door. "Stand up."

"You drug me and then complain that I can't stand up. How dumb are you?" It was hard to get her mouth to work.

"Shut up, Sara."

Sara's knees buckled, and Regina let her fall in a heap on the floor. Her head cracked against the wood, and it felt like an earthquake rattling her brain. It was already hard to keep her eyes open, and the fall had knocked the wind out of her and made it hard to think. Her side and hip pulsed as pain rippled through her.

She groaned as she blinked, trying to clear her head. Liam. Her mom couldn't hurt him.

After taking a few deep breaths, she rolled her head and looked at Regina. "You're so stupid. If you were a man, I'd demand a paternity test."

"Shut up, Sara." Her mom waived the gun at Liam. "I'll shoot him."

"It's a miracle you don't have to wear headphones that tell you when to breathe in and out." Sara chuckled. She needed her mom to get angry. To point that gun at her.

Her mom scoffed. "I know he has a thing for you. You can't fool me."

"You think he could love someone like me? Someone who came from something like you? What did I do to deserve you as a mother?" Sara laughed. Her mouth was dry and sticky, and it was getting harder to stay awake.

Her mom growled and pointed the gun at her. "I said be quiet. Liam and I have some things to discuss."

"Like what? He's my client. Have I ever crossed a line with a client before?" She hadn't, and her mom knew that.

"Clients don't take their employees to things like what I saw."

What could she do now? She tipped her head back and looked at Liam. "Fine, so he took me. You think he's the kind of guy to settle down? With me? How many other women has he taken to something like that?" She looked at her mom again. "Think about it, you idiot. He's a billionaire. Women are like candy packs in a vending machine to someone like him."

She tipped her head back and looked him. The hurt in his eyes made her chest tighten.

"Sara?" His voice was soft.

Regina's lip curled up. "I hate you. Do you know that? I have hated you from the moment you stepped into my life. I had a good thing going, and then you came along. I wish I'd never had you."

"And you think you win Mother of the Year? You're a pathetic excuse for a human being. You'll never be anything. I'll always be better than you." Sara hoped that last dig would push Regina over the edge. Maybe it would give Liam time to run or something. Hopefully, he wouldn't get hurt.

Sara closed her eyes as she saw her mom pull the trigger, and then she heard a click. She opened her eyes when it clicked again and again. "Did you not put bullets in it?"

"I bought it from Chris. He said he put bullets in it."

"You bought a gun from someone dumb enough to blow twenty million dollars in six months? And beat me up over a hundred bucks? Do you think he'd give you anything for free? Geez. You really are stupid." She laughed loud and hard.

Like something out of a movie, the door behind her mom opened, and two large men dressed in black poured in. They grabbed Regina and took the gun from her.

Liam raced to Sara and knelt next to her. "Are you hurt?"

"I don't know."

He cradled her in his arms. "Did she drug you?"

She nodded. "S-sleeping pills, but it could be poison slowly killing me. There's really no telling." Finally, she was safe again.

He scooped her up. "We need to get her to the emergency room."

"I'll drive," Kimberly said.

Sara felt Liam's breath on her cheek.

"Stay awake, okay?"

It was the last thing she heard.

∾

LIAM PUSHED Sara's hair back from her face and ran his fingers down the length of it. When they'd arrived at the emergency room, her stomach had been pumped. Lucky for her, her mom hadn't wanted to poison her, and she'd only been given some strong sleeping pills. The fall to the floor hadn't given her a concussion, but if she didn't wake up with a headache, he'd be surprised.

When he'd received her text, he was hoping she'd changed her mind. The private investigator he'd hired called right after and told him that something seemed off. The moment her car had started up the mountain, he'd called the security he'd hired. He wasn't sure what was going to happen, but Kimberly had convinced him to take no chances. He was glad he'd listened to his sister.

"How's she doing?" Kim asked.

He didn't take his eyes off Sara as he answered. "Sleeping it off."

"Why are you so down? I thought you'd be happy she's back." Kimberly laid her hand on his arm.

Looking at her, he shook his head. "She thinks of me as a client. You heard her, what she thinks about me."

Kimberly rolled her eyes. "Oh, baby brother, I love

you, but sometimes you can be so thick. Would you like to hear my version of events?"

How was he being thick? "Sure."

"I saw a woman who promised to take care of you, drugged with her hands bound, lying on the floor and hurling insults at a woman who had a gun trained on you, who then pointed it at her. And that woman fired it, or tried. Think, Liam."

Realization hit him.

"There we go. Turn that light bulb on." She smiled.

"You think that's what was really going on?" he asked as he looked back down at Sara.

She nodded. "Yeah, I really do."

"I guess I need to have a talk with her when she wakes up."

"You want me to stay?" his sister asked as she touched his arm.

He looked at her and shook his head. "No, you go home. I'm fine here."

"Okay, call me if you need me. That goes for her too." She smiled and patted his shoulder.

Liam nodded. "Thanks."

His sister walked out, and the door clicked shut behind her. He sat beside Sara and kissed her forehead. If she loved him half as much as he loved her, he wasn't letting her go again.

CHAPTER 26

*L*iam jerked awake and looked in Sara's direction. She was moving for the first time since he'd brought her to the hospital some ten hours ago. He stood from the chair he'd napped in and strode to the bed, taking a seat beside her.

"Hi," she whispered and licked her lips.

Liam grabbed the cup of water off the little table next to the bed, filled it with water from the pitcher, and lifted her so she could have a drink. He filled it twice more before she put her hand up, signaling she was good at the moment.

"A little thirsty." He chuckled.

She nodded. "My mouth was dry and sticky. And I feel like I'm coming out of a fog."

"Do you remember anything?"

"Mostly. My mom wanted to meet. Said she was sorry for the way she'd treated me. We talked a bit, and she asked if I wanted to see her apartment. I never even left the table. I don't know how she drugged me." She raked her hand through her hair and winced. "My head hurts."

"She knew the waitress at the restaurant," Liam said. The private investigator he'd hired did a full background check on her mom and anyone she might be associated with.

She looked at him. "What?"

"Your mom gave the waitress the drugs, and she put them in your drink." Liam paused. "She's in pretty big trouble. Your mom is too. She's not walking away this time."

She smiled. "Good."

"What else do you remember?" He was most curious about the next part.

Her eyes closed. "I remember...seeing you. She had a gun pointed at you, and I didn't want her to shoot you. I knew if I made her mad enough she'd point it at me."

His eyebrows drew together. "How did you know it wasn't loaded?"

"I didn't." She said it so casually, like it was no big deal she'd risked her life.

His pulse jumped. "What?"

She opened her eyes and looked at him. "I had no idea. I just knew I'd promised Kimberly I'd take care of you. And then I fell in love with you, and the promise didn't have an expiration date anymore."

He looked at her, unable to believe his ears. She loved him? "You love me?"

"I love you with all my heart."

Liam felt like he'd been hit with a bat. "If you love me, why did you leave me?"

She touched his knee. "I had to. You didn't know my mom or what she was capable of, and I thought if I left you'd be safe. I didn't realize she'd seen us at the event in California. It never even occurred to me that she'd see it."

"I told you I had ways to take care of myself."

Sara looked down. "It wasn't a risk I was willing to take."

He leaned across her and braced his hand on the bed. "So, all that stuff about other women and vending machines?"

She shrugged. "If she thought you cared about me, she'd have blackmailed you or whatever else she could think of."

"I more than care about you. I love you."

Her gaze lifted and locked with his. "You do?"

"Sara, I love you with all that's in me." He bent down and kissed her.

She scooted over and patted the bed. "Think you can hold me for a while?"

"I think I can do better than a while." He lay down next to her and put his arms around her.

With her head tilted up, looking at him, he brushed her hair back and swept his fingers across her cheek. "Marry me."

She sat up and looked at him. "Are you serious? We've known each other for a month."

"The way I see it, if I can't make forever work with you, then I've got no hope with anyone else."

Her lips parted. "You *are* serious."

He nodded. "Yeah, I am."

She settled herself back in the crook of his arm. The clock on the wall ticked louder than any he'd ever heard. If she said no, he was going to wait and ask again in a few months. He'd keep asking until she said yes.

"So, will you marry me?" he asked.

"Yes."

He almost thought he was hearing things. "Yes?"

"Unless you were kidding."

"I wasn't kidding." He pulled a little box from his

pocket and opened it. "I bought this at the same time I bought the necklace."

Her lips parted in a gasp. "You did?"

"The trip to California was my love letter to you. I'm head over heels in love with you, Sara." He paused. "And the necklace is at the house. I found it in my luggage. When we get home, you can take it back."

She caught her bottom lip between her teeth. "I didn't want my mom getting her hands on it, and I knew she'd find a way to take it."

As he leaned down to kiss her, he slipped the ring on her finger. She circled her arms around his neck and slid her fingers into his hair.

LIAM HAD his arms around her, kissing her, and the weight of a piece of jewelry had never felt lighter. She'd already promised to take care of him; now she could promise to love him too.

She broke the kiss and pulled back. "My mom isn't going to hurt you? You weren't just saying that?"

He shook his head. "No, she's in trouble. I'm pressing charges against her. She trespassed, aimed a weapon at me, and then fired with the intent to hurt you. Bullets or no, the intent was there. Plus, she drugged you. She's done."

"It feels wrong to say it, but I'm so relieved. She's all the family I had, and I was holding on, hoping she'd one day love me." She sighed.

Liam smiled. "Actually, that's not true. You have grandparents who've been itching to meet you."

"I do?"

"Regina's parents. They tried to get custody of you when your dad died, but your mom wouldn't let them have you. Then she moved, and they couldn't find you."

Her eyes went wide, and her jaw dropped. "How do you know all this?"

He scrunched up his face. "I had a private investigator look into your mom. I hope you aren't mad."

She smiled. "No, that's great. They want to meet me?"

"According to the detective, yes."

"I would like that." She kissed him. "Thank you." She had grandparents who wanted her and a man who loved and wanted her. It was an incredible feeling. "You have no idea how much I love you."

He smiled. "I might have a tiny idea."

He leaned to kiss her, and she put a finger to his lips.

"Why were you so mean to me that day? What had happened?" she asked.

"I started having feelings for you, and it scared me. It was the only thing I could think of to stop it. To make you so angry you wouldn't have anything to do with me."

"That was the reason?"

"All that insight, and you didn't figure that out?" He smiled.

She shook her head. "No, but it hurt me more than it should have, so that should have been a clue."

"I'm sorry."

Her lips curved into a smile. "You've more than made up for it." Her face fell. "But what does your sister think about this? I mean, she hired me to be your nurse. I think this is a little more than she bargained for."

"She loves me, and I love you."

She pulled her bottom lip in and chewed it. "Okay."

Liam leaned in and kissed her, taking her lip between his teeth and letting go. "Every time you do that, I'm going to kiss you."

Sara ran her fingers through his beard and touched her forehead to his.

"And that."

She brushed her lips along his jaw and swept them

across his face until she found his lips. He immediately deepened the kiss and squeezed her to him. Her body melted against his. Their lips moved together, and hours later, flushed and breathing hard, they broke apart.

"Set a date," Liam said.

"Tomorrow," she said as she nuzzled his neck.

He chuckled. "I'm serious."

"Six months."

"Somewhere in between?" He kissed her throat.

"How about as soon as I find a dress and meet my grandparents?"

"It's a deal."

EPILOGUE

Three months later...

"Cover your eyes," Liam said.

Sara tilted her head. "Why?"

"Just do it."

They'd said their vows a few hours ago and were getting ready to leave the reception for their honeymoon. After three months of waiting, he was her husband, and she'd never been happier.

She looked at him and pursed her lips. "Fine." Her hands covered her eyes, and she wondered what he could possibly be up to. He was the most incredibly sweet man.

He took her shoulders, guiding her until they were outside in the evening air.

"What have you done, Liam?"

Standing behind her, he took her wrists and pulled her hands from her eyes. "Goosey?" It came out breathless, and tears pooled in her eyes.

Her old car had been transformed. She was a beautiful dark blue with white interior and rims that looked straight from the factory. It was like he'd stepped through a time machine and brought her back. She was perfect.

"Well, mostly. The body was too far gone, and it couldn't be saved, but Mike salvaged as much from Goosey as he could. I know it's not—"

It was Goosey. He'd brought her back. She spun on her heels, wrapped her arms around him, and kissed him. "I can't believe you did this."

"You love her, and I love you. I thought we'd drive her to Dallas and take a plane from there. I know you've missed her." He smiled.

Sara took his face in her hands. "You are the sweetest man I've ever known. That you would do this for me...I can't begin to tell you what it means to me, or how much I love you."

"I love your smile, and I'm making it my mission in life to see your smile as much as possible." He picked her up around the waist and kissed her. "I love you, Mrs. Thomas."

She hugged him around the neck. "I love you, Mr. Thomas."

A Clean Fake Relationship Romance Book Two

The Bodyguard's Fake Marriage:
A Clean Fake Relationship Romance Book Three

The Matchmaker's Fake Marriage:
A Clean Fake Relationship Romance Book Four

The Beast's Fake Marriage:
A Clean Fake Relationship Romance Book Five

A Clean Army Ranger Romance Series:

The Ranger's Chance:
A Clean Army Ranger Romance Book One

The Ranger's Peace:
A Clean Army Ranger Romance Book Two

The Ranger's Heart:
A Clean Army Ranger Romance Book Three

The Ranger's Hope:
A Clean Army Ranger Romance Book Four

Clean Stand Alone Romances:

Love and Charity

The Mistletoe Game:

A Clean Christmas Novella

ABOUT THE AUTHOR

Bree Livingston lives in the West Texas Panhandle with her husband, children, and cats. She'd have a dog, but they took a vote and the cats won. Not in numbers, but attitude. They wouldn't even debate. They just leveled their little beady eyes at her and that was all it took for her to nix getting a dog. Her hobbies include...nothing because she writes all the time.

She loves carbs, but the love ends there. No, that's not true. The love usually winds up on her hips which is why she loves writing romance. The love in the pages of her books are sweet and clean, and they definitely don't add pounds when you step on the scale. Unless of course, you're actually holding a Kindle while you're weighing. Put the Kindle down and try again. Also, the cookie because that could be the problem too. She knows from experience.

Join her mailing list to be the first to find out publishing news, contests, and more by going to her website at https://www.breelivingston.com.